To Laressa,

Enjoy the Book!

Lindorff Frank

# The Mystery
### *of the*
# Lost Avenger

## OTHER ANNIE TILLERY MYSTERIES BY THE AUTHOR

The Madonna Ghost
Girl with Pencil, Drawing
Secrets in the Fairy Chimneys

# The Mystery
## *of the*
# Lost Avenger

Linda Maria Frank

ARCHWAY
PUBLISHING

Archway Publishing books may be ordered through booksellers or by contacting:

Archway Publishing
1663 Liberty Drive
Bloomington, IN 47403
www.archwaypublishing.com
1 (888) 242-5904

ISBN: 978-1-4808-3169-8 (sc)
ISBN: 978-1-4808-3167-4 (hc)
ISBN: 978-1-4808-3168-1 (e)

Library of Congress Control Number: 2016909439

Print information available on the last page.

Archway Publishing rev. date: 6/14/2016

# REVIEWS

The **Madonna Ghost** is a great way to introduce Young Adult readers to the often convoluted world of science. It is easy to confuse a fictional TV show such as CSI with reality. Linda Frank does use an element of science to tell the story, but much prefers good old common sense. http://www.bloggernews.net/134804

What jumped out at me while reading **Girl With Pencil, Drawing** was the close attention paid to detail. No art forger worth his or her salt forges a well-known work, trying to sell a copy of the Mona Lisa, would likely not get very far in the art world. Forgers tend to go for lesser known artists. A good forger does not copy, he creates a new as yet undiscovered work by an artist. The master forger will even go so far as to weave a fictitious provenance for the work.

Linda Frank touches on all of these subjects and much more. Although billed as a YA (Young Adult) book I think it has much broader appeal. http://www.bloggernews.net/134885

For **Secrets in the Fairy Chimneys** I rather like the style that the author uses, she does not talk down to her young readers, rather she treats them as peers on a quest.

I had the opportunity to talk to Linda before reading her latest book. It is amazing how much you can learn about a book before you read it. "CSI meets Nancy Drew" was a comment that I rather liked. Indeed Annie Tillery is much more modern than Nancy Drew. The writing style is also much more modern. http://www.bloggernews.net/134466

From Cold Coffee Press on Amazon
http://www.amazon.com/Pencil-Drawing-Linda-Maria-Frank-ebook/dp/B00QWD2WA0/ref=asap_bc?ie=UTF8
With strong characters, flowing dialog and layers of mystery, soon everyone is caught up in a real who-dun-it that involves a long lists of suspects and hidden clues. Twists and turns with all the dangers that come into play when an International Art Fraud has been perpetrated. Learn the ins and out of the art world that include how scientists tests for authenticity in original paintings by world renown artist like Renoir and the lucrative forgeries that make this underworld as treacherous as any international mob association.

Follow the clues, wait for the DNA evidence and sift through the ashes left by an arsonist. Inspire a young reader to discover the innate detective skills of Annie Tillery who is fast becoming the next Nancy Drew. This series should be placed on our schools' summer reading list.

Cold Coffee Press endorses '**Girl with Pencil, Drawing**' and the Annie Tillery Mysteries by Linda Maria Frank. We received a PDF version of this book for review. Review completion date March 24, 2015. For more information please visit Cold Coffee Press.

http://www.amazon.com/Secrets-Fairy-Chimneys-Linda-Maria-ebook/dp/B00IUQ7WZC/ref=asap_bc?ie=UTF8

Bravo to Linda Maria Frank! This third book in her Annie Tillery Mystery series is a stunner! Although written for a YA audience, even I as a senior citizen was captured by the mystery and intrigue interwoven throughout this story. And who could resist the element of romance embedded in the two oh-so-appealing main characters, Annie and Ty? But most compelling to me was an introduction to the history and topography of this country with its ancient **Fairy Chimneys**. Half way through this book, I began researching trips to this wonderland and have placed Turkey at the top of my bucket list for future travels. A beautifully crafted, impeccably edited work. Linda Maria Frank deserves many kudos and an equal number of followers. I know I will be looking out for more of her books to recommend to the young adults in my life, but not before I sneak a peek at them myself.

Lois W. Stern
Creator of the Tales2Inspire book series
http://www.amazon.com/review/RQ5GFVPOJDAL8/ref=cm_cr_dp_title?ie=UTF8&ASIN=1491710624&channel=detail-glance&nodeID=283155&store=books

**A Page-Turning Mystery and Great Summer Read!**
*The Madonna Ghost: An Annie Tillery Mystery* By Karen Bonnet, author of *Whale Island and the Mysterious Bones*.

This riveting story, set on beautiful, historic Fire Island, takes readers on a page-turning adventure that begins with protagonist/teenager Annie Tillery and her NYPD detective, Aunt Jill. While vacationing on Fire Island during the summer, Annie, a likeable teenager with an unstable family life, finds romance and uncovers a sinister plot with newfound boyfriend, Ty Egan. Together, they discover why a local ghost has been "appearing" for years and causing concern among the townspeople who have seen her walking along the shores of the beach, searching for her long-lost child. Annie and Ty soon learn that Aunt Jill's difficult and hostile neighbors may be the reason for her aunt's sudden disappearance. While the plot thickens and readers become more entrenched in the lives of the characters, Linda Maria Frank continues to weave her intriguing and captivating adventure/mystery that keeps readers on the edge of their seats!

Patricia Roberts, 5th Grade Teacher, Stewart School, Garden City, N.Y. writes:

I am glad to have the opportunity to write a few words regarding The Annie Tillery Mystery series written by Linda Maria Frank. My 5th grade students have used all of her books for different books clubs. They thoroughly enjoyed reading about how Annie solved her mysteries. Their group discussions were rich and engaging. They analyzed Annie's character traits, made predictions and even discussed the importance of each book cover. Because of these books, many students wanted to learn more about forensic science. In addition, the students chose to use her books as mentor texts for writing their own mysteries. The 'fan favorites' were **The Madonna Ghost** and **Secrets in the Fairy Chimneys**. It is difficult sometimes to find a book series that both boys and girls enjoy reading – but Linda's books appealed to both groups of students.

I have encourage many of my colleagues to read her books as either a read aloud to discuss text features (character development, setting etc) or as book club choices. My students continue to enjoy her books and are very excited to learn that **The Mystery of the Lost Avenger** will soon be available for them to read!

Patricia Roberts, 5th Grade Teacher, Stewart School, Garden City, N.Y.

## ACKNOWLEDGEMENTS

This is a book of fiction. Yes, WWII happened and the Grumman plant on Long Island that produced the Avenger are factual. Republic Field in Farmingdale is a thriving commercial airport. The apprehension of German spies in Amagansett is also in the historical record. All other elements of plot, setting and character are inventions of the author.

Thanks to the curators of the Cradle of Aviation Museum in Garden City, Long Island, Josh Stoff and Julia Lauria-Blum, for their help in providing materials from their archives, a vast treasure trove of information about Long Island's role in WWII. Kudos go to my editor, Matt Pasca, for his attention to detail, helping get my story to the reader in its best possible form.

This work is dedicated to my Muses and personal historians: Angie, Edie, Connie, Mildred and Maxine

# CONTENTS

# PROLOGUE

## *The Dangers of Flying Solo*

Carol Wheeler sat in her car on a suburban street in New Windsor, Maryland. Her hand shook as she read the letter from the Department of the Navy for perhaps the twentieth time. It concerned something they had discovered about her grandmother's role in World War II. The Navy had found a note in the wreckage of a plane that crashed in 1943, recently recovered in Appalachia. The note was traced to Charlotte Wheeler, Carol's grandmother. Why had her grandmother put a note in a fighter plane that was being flown by someone else to a California air base? Charlotte had not been flying that plane. She did not die in 1943.

Carol pulled into the driveway of the home she grew up in and stared at it, memories of her childhood and school days flooding back. *Maybe I can find something in the attic that will shed some light on this mystery. After all she did live here.* Carol tucked the letter into her purse, shivering at the idea of entering that attic. Fishing in her purse, she pulled out the keys she needed to get into both the house, now occupied by a tenant, and the attic. *I feel like a sneak thief,* she thought. *I'll leave a note for Tallie. I don't want her to think I snoop around here at will. I did send her a note.* "Darn it! Why do I feel so guilty? I own this place," she said, slamming the car door.

Gathering her resolve, Carol fumbled with the keys, finally selecting the correct one and entered the house by the side door, made her way to the second floor, and unlocked the door to the attic stairs.

"It smells the same. Probably nobody has touched a thing here since I put Mom in the nursing home. They're going to put me in the loony bin if I don't stop talking to myself."

The heat in the attic produced a sheen of sweat all over Carol's body, making her a bit light-headed. *I'll have to get out of here fast,* she thought, propping the door open.

"Good. The trunks are where I remember them. Before she died, Mom told me all the family mementos are packed inside of them."

Carol approached the trunks. Two were stained oak with barrel tops, bound in brass straps. The hardware was beginning to show signs of rust. The third one was a maroon steamer trunk, the kind used by immigrants bound for America on ocean liners. This was the one she opened. A strong smell of cinnamon and cloves rose from it. Inside were packets of letters. She scooped them up, and put them in her tote. The second trunk held picture albums. "It's too much to carry. I'll have to come back with someone."

Curiosity got the best of her and Carol lifted a few framed pictures, turning them to the light from the single bare bulb. She gasped. The young woman in the one photo that fell out of the group looked back at her like a mirror image. The photograph was signed in the bottom right corner, *Charlotte*. *My grandmother*, Carol mused. *That could just as well be me*, she thought.

The door to the attic slammed, making Carol jump and clutch the photos to her chest.

"Who's there?"

Carol ran to the door, pulling at it. It was stuck. She put the photos on a bureau and pulled at the knob with all her might. The door opened, nearly toppling her to the floor. She looked down the long hall where the door to the rest of the house stood open. A woman with a carefully pinned up-do of blonde curls, in a knee-length floral print dress was heading to the floor below.

"Tallie, is that you? Wait! Who is that? What are you doing in my house?"

There was no answer. The photo of Charlotte popped into Carol's head. She shook herself to clear that vision, her hands trembling.

"That's impossible," she whispered. She put the photos back in the trunk, grabbed her tote, and ran out of the house.

Heart pounding, Carol dropped the keys as she tried to lock the door.

Safely inside her car, she said, "What in the world was THAT? *I'm not coming here alone again*, she thought. Turning to the house, she muttered, "I don't believe in ghosts, but did I just see one?"

A door slammed somewhere on the second floor below us.
"I'll go see who it is," I said. At the end of the hallway a
woman in a flowered dress, hair done up on top of her head
was going through another door, slamming it behind her.

# CHAPTER 1

## *Annie Bumps into the Past*

"No! No! No! Stop that!" My still nameless kitten was dragging my brand -new cashmere sweater out of the box I had carefully packed it in.

"Come here." As I lunged for the tiny ball of fur whose sharp little teeth clenched the sweater, she backpedaled away from me. I almost had her when she rolled over, tangling the claws of all four paws in the soft blue wool.

"You are killing my sweater," I shrieked.

The sweater got up and ran toward my room. That sweater was a gift from my boyfriend, Ty. I hadn't even worn the thing. Heading to the kitchen, I thought, just maybe, I could lure Nameless close enough to grab her. I found a bag of treats and, rattling them in what I thought was a most appealing way, entered the bedroom.

The doorbell rang followed by the vibration of the phone in my pocket. I made a desperate attempt to answer the phone,

1

before it stopped, as I headed for the door. Caller ID registered my Aunt Jill, better known as Detective Jill Tillery, NYPD.

"Hi, Aunt J. Can you hold? Someone's at the door."

"Annie, look through the peephole before you open."

I rolled my eyes. "Yes, Aunt J. I've already activated the jars of boiling oil over the door in case it's one of your bad guys."

"Ha ha." The tinny laugh buzzed from the phone.

But I fell into the time worn habit and looked through the peephole. I fumbled with the two deadlocks and threw open the door.

"Dad, what are you doing here? I thought you were in Istanbul."

He wrapped his arms around me, and we shared a big hug.

"Annie," he said, a note of curiosity in his voice. "What's that?" I followed his gaze to the ball of blue cashmere skittering down the hall toward us.

"Aww," I cooed. Nameless was meowing pitifully. I guess the novelty of being imprisoned in my sweater had worn off. "It's a kitten, Dad."

"Oh," was all he could manage.

Come on in. I'll make us a snack."

I picked up my little trouble maker and we went down the hall to the apartment's kitchen. I sat at the table and, as Dad looked on, tried to minimize the damage to the sweater while I freed the kitten. She stood up and rubbed against my hand. My heart melted as she curled into the crook of my arm, purring louder than her size should allow.

Nameless looked up at me, contentedly blinking her yellow-green eyes. She was gray with a white underbelly and paws. Her face had a white blaze between her eyes, extending to a ring around her mouth. She looked like she had fallen face first into a dish of vanilla ice cream. To complete her ensemble, her bushy tail was tipped in white.

"Dad, can you hold her while I make some coffee?"

"How about that chair cushion over there," he replied, looking very reluctant. "I see what she's done to your sweater. I kind of like these jeans."

"Okay, okay." As I lifted her to the chair, Nameless squeaked in protest and bounded back to the living room.

"I need a name for her," I said, as I spooned coffee into the percolator. No automatic machine for us. My Aunt Jill was a purist when it came to coffee. After all her years working as an NYPD detective, she claimed that good coffee came only from a real percolator with boiling water.

I lived with my Aunt Jill, since Dad worked out of the country, and my mother was recovering from a substance abuse problem.

"Coffee smells good, Annie. Why not call the cat Trouble . . . or Destructo?"

"C'mon, she's not that bad. Look at her. She's adorable!" The cat, of course, was nowhere to be seen.

I set out two mugs, sugar, half and half. I opened a tin of chocolate chip cookies and sat down across from Randall, my father.

"Are you all packed for school, Honey?"

"Well, you saw the living room." I motioned to the chaotic arrangement of boxes and electronics, blankets, bedding, books, snowboard, and other items I deemed necessary to take. It seemed perfectly clear to me that I needed to be ready for any situation Vermont University might present. I'm starting my first year there as a Biology major. This apartment was big, but apparently not big enough for my move to college. "The bedroom is worse. I haven't seen the bed for days."

"Are you nervous about moving up to Vermont?" Dad asked, with a directness that was very much his style. It had put me on the spot many times in my life.

"Dad, I am *so* excited. Ty will be there and his best friend, Cedric. This is what I want." I smiled at him, hugging myself to keep from jumping up and down.

I poured the coffee and took a bite of cookie. Almost choking, I remembered, "Oh, Aunt Jill. I have to call her back."

"She's . . ." Dad's comment was cut off by the sound of the apartment door opening and Aunt J's call from the foyer, "It's me."

"Aunt J, I was just going to call you back."

Dad stood and embraced Aunt J before pulling me in for a group hug.

"How's the NYPD, Jill?" Dad asked.

"People still killin' and robbin' and beatin' each other up. But we keep the racket down to a dull roar. How's everything at State?" she replied.

My dad worked for the State Department, specifically at its office in Istanbul, Turkey. He laughed. "You know, it sounds just like what I deal with, only in a different language."

They shook their heads.

"Done packing?" Aunt Jill asked me, winking at Dad. "And, what has that cat destroyed today?" she said, causing Dad to choke on his cookie.

These were my two favorite people in the whole world, next to Ty, my boyfriend. My dad was not bad to look at. His sandy hair was graying a bit, but his tall frame was still fit enough to show off his jeans and pullover to their best advantage. His blue eyes sparkled as he shared a knowing look with Aunt J. He was as tall as she was petite, but their coloring and facial features were a DNA match. I was tall and strong like my dad, my own hair a few shades blonder. I missed the blue eyes of both my mom and dad, getting some recessive set of genes that made my eyes green.

Aunt Jill poured a cup of coffee and sat down, looking at me with an expression I knew so well. Something was coming that I wasn't so sure I wanted to hear.

"I'll get the packing done. . . soon," I offered.

Jill held up her hand, shaking her head. She and Dad focused on me. "Something has come up, Annie," Jill said.

*Oh, no,* I thought. *My college acceptance fell through. Oh God, was Ty in an accident?* I must have gone very pale, because Jill clasped my hand and Dad pulled his chair closer.

# CHAPTER 2

## C Cubed: Carol, Carla and Charlotte

"Nothing bad, Honey," Dad said. "Its something interesting about your Mom's family history. It's a lot to explain. Mom forwarded a copy of a letter she got from the investigative branch of the U.S. Navy."

"Oh, Mom." I tried to keep the hollow sound out of my voice. I didn't get along so well with Mom. She has a serious substance abuse problem, mostly drinking. She was not there for a lot of my childhood. She'd been sober for about four years though, and we'd been trying to build a relationship. "Still, it was uncomfortable for me. I felt like if I said the wrong thing she might pick up a drink. That's a big responsibility, one I mostly tried to avoid. I knew it hurt her, but she hurt me for years. I hated this.

"It's about her grandmother, your great-grandmother. Did Carol ever tell you anything about her?" Dad asked. I found it strange when he referred to Mom as Carol.

"Not really. Was she famous or something?" I studied the ring my coffee cup made on the kitchen table, not sure I wanted to hear what they had to say.

"I'll tell you what I can, and Mom will give you all the details when she comes."

I didn't know what to think or feel as Dad launched into the story.

"Carol's mother, Carla Wheeler, was a regular 1960's housewife. I always got the impression that she was disappointed with her life, that she wanted to do more. She once told me that her mother, Charlotte Wheeler, had led a very exciting life working as a pilot in a defense plant during World War II."

"That's strange," I said. "They all have the same last name. Shouldn't that have changed with their marriages?"

"According to Carol, they decided to start a tradition of keeping their own family name. Your mother goes by Carol Wheeler," J explained.

"But not me," I said. "I'm a Tillery."

"At my insistence," Dad replied. "I had custody of you for most of your childhood. I just found it easier."

What he meant was he never knew if Mom would survive her love affair with Jack Daniels and the occasional narcotic.

"Okay, so what in the world did great-gramma-what's-her-name have to do with the Navy?" I asked.

"Read this," Dad insisted. He handed me a copy of the letter from the Navy. I read it, scanning for pertinent details.

*Dear Ms. Wheeler-Tillery:*

*We have recovered a note we believe to have been written by your grandmother, Charlotte Wheeler, who was an employee of Grumman Aviation, and a WASP (Women's Airforce Service Pilots) between 1942 and 1945. The note was found on an official Grumman form used by the plant workers in Building 3, where Avenger aircraft were manufactured.*

*Further, the note was found in the wreckage of an Avenger aircraft that we believe crashed on its way to the naval base in California where it would have been loaded on an aircraft carrier headed for the Pacific.*

*Our records show that the plane was lost, until discovered by a mining company team in West Virginia in October of 2014.*

*The wreckage is being investigated by NCIS and NTSB, as is the origin of the note. We will keep you apprised of the progress of our investigation, and would like to question you about Charlotte Wheeler at your earliest convenience.*

*Yours respectfully,*

*Capt. Carl Boyle, NCIS*


A note found in the wreckage was traced to Charlotte. *What did this mean? How was my great-grandmother involved in this crash?* I thought.

The air in the room was too warm all of a sudden. I didn't think finding out about my ancestors would be so emotional. Tears welled in my eyes and I slumped in the nearest chair. A vision of my great-grandmother, sitting in the cockpit of a plane, looking at a piece of paper appeared unbidden on my mind's TV screen. I shook my head to clear that picture.

Dad was standing over me. "Are you okay, Annie?"

"This is so strange, Dad. I had sort of a flashback or something. What do you know about Charlotte?"

"Charlotte worked for Grumman Aviation, building, and eventually flying a plane called the Avenger. It played a prominent role in winning World War II," Dad filled in.

"And you'll love this part, Annie," Jill added. "So many men were fighting the war overseas that women were hired by the defense companies to build tanks, planes and other equipment used to fight the war. Did any of your history teachers ever talk about Rosie the Riveter?"

"Sure. We did a whole unit about the changing role of women in the 20th century, and there was a lot of material about Rosie the Riveter. Wow! So my great- grandmother was one of those plane builders?"

"Not only did she build 'em, she flew 'em." Aunt Jill smiled, warming to the subject and enjoying a moment of feminine pride.

"Flew them in the war?" I gasped.

"No. The planes needed to be delivered to the air bases where the pilots trained. The Navy couldn't spare the airmen, so they trained some of the Rosies, who later became WASPS, which stands for Women's Airforce Service Pilots. They flew the planes to California."

"I guess that assured they built a plane with no mistakes. They had to fly them!" It was a lot to take in. *My great-grand-mother, wearing one of those tight leather helmet, and goofy goggles, flying through the clouds, acting as a test pilot for a brand new war plane.* "Jeez, and I got this lady's genes."

Dad broke in, "Do you want to read her note?"

"Yeah, why would she leave a note in the plane?"

He handed me another sheet of paper. I was glad to get these pieces of the puzzle one at a time. I wanted to have time to get their meaning.

The note said:

*I tested your plane. I hope my note's a lucky charm, Fly Boy. Make sure you check those bomb bay doors.*

This was followed by a string of numbers.

"I guess she left the note for the pilots? But why did she ask him to check the bomb bay doors? And what do these numbers mean?" I looked from Dad to Aunt J.

Dad raised his eyebrows and said in a somber tone, "The Navy is investigating this crash, because it's one of the few Avengers to crash where they can actually check the bomb bay doors. The ones that went down in combat could not be investigated. The Navy wants to see if there was some sort of sabotage, partly because of the note, and partly because the plane went missing in 1943 with no explanation."

"After all these years?" I said.

"After all these years," he replied.

"And why did they send this information to you?"

"It was really sent to Carol, and she asked me to explain it to you. She's gone to the family home in New Windsor, Maryland to see what she can dig up. She said her mother never threw anything away. She might find something to shed light on this mystery."

# CHAPTER 3

## The Last Flight of Avenger # 3008

June 12, 1943

*At 6AM, the sun made* a brief appearance on the horizon before hiding behind the cloud bank building to the east. Somewhere in that direction, ships carrying troops and supplies to the Allies in Europe were being preyed upon by German U-boats- a wolf pack that sought to destroy the Allies' effort to win the war.

The tarmac was damp with the night's deposit of dew and the air smelled of the Atlantic Ocean only a few miles away. No wind, no rain, especially to the west where newly built planes were headed to U.S. Navy pilots who would fly them to win the war in the Pacific.

"Charlotte Wheeler," the dispatcher known as Sarge called out.

A tall woman in a brown flight suit hefting a messenger bag moved toward the plane indicated by Sarge's outstretched hand.

"Sign here. Charlotte Wheeler, right?"

"You forgot who I am?" Charlotte mumbled sarcastically. "I need to check a few things, Sarge."

Charlotte completed a walk around the plane, pausing by the wing on the left side. She climbed up on the wing, fished in her pocket for something, slid into the cockpit like the pro she was, and came out about thirty seconds later. Charlotte knew everything there was to know about the Avenger. She had built them and flown them to the west coast naval base where they were loaded onto aircraft carriers that would take the planes and the pilots trained to fly them to fight the Japanese fleet.

"I'm going inside for a minute. I have to check something I found," Charlotte called over her shoulder to Sarge.

"You'll lose your place," he called back.

"Just one minute!"

Charlotte disappeared into the hangar and Sarge called out, "Brenda McPhee!"

Brenda walked up, crossed out Charlotte's name, replaced it with her own signature, and against her training, did an incomplete check of the plane. She trusted that Charlotte's inspection was good enough. All of this took three minutes. Brenda climbed into the cockpit. By the time she finished a quick cockpit check and fastened her seatbelt, Charlotte had not reappeared.

The grounds man pulled out the wheel chocks and gave Brenda the signal to go. As Brenda taxied toward the runway, Charlotte emerged from the hangar. When she heard the roar of her plane speeding down the runway, she looked for Sarge. She saw him talking to a guy in civilian clothes, a dark suit and a fedora pulled low, showing only his profile. Sarge said something to the suit and he turned away, walking briskly to the exit. Sarge saw Charlotte and she gave him a hard look. He, too, turned away. Brenda and the plane were never seen or heard from again.

# CHAPTER 4

## *Who Was Charlotte Wheeler?*

"Hi, Ty, it's Annie. Call when u can." I texted. There was too much to explain in a text, and I wanted to hear his voice.

Tucking the phone in my pocket, I stared at the mountain of boxes, duffels and suitcases in the hallway. My packing was finally done. I still had two weeks before heading up to Vermont for the start of the fall semester. I'd been lucky enough to rent a cute little apartment in the private home of one of Aunt J's friends, Doc Egan. He was also Ty's uncle. Aunt J and I once spent a couple of weeks with Doc and Ty at Doc's summer home on Fire Island. That's where I met Ty.

I sat in the kitchen waiting for Mom. She had returned from New Windsor where, she claimed, she'd discovered a treasure trove of Charlotte's belongings. I walked to the living room where the kitten, now known as Trouble, was sleeping on a wide window seat. I was going to pet her, but thought the better of it. If I woke her, she'd do some crazy thing, and

I didn't want to be distracted from what my mother might bring.

I heard a tentative knock on the door, and the bell rang. I could see her through the peephole. She was carrying a red plastic tote fairly bursting at the seams. I opened the door and she entered, limping under the weight of the tote. With a whoosh of exhaled breath, she put the tote down and smiled at me.

"Hi, Mom." We air kissed. Without a real hug from me, she looked away with that beaten dog face. I felt guilty. It was always like this. Maybe someday one of us would be able to overcome the past and just act naturally.

"Look at all that stuff!" Having recovered, she glanced around the room. "Is it all going to Vermont? Are you ever coming back?"

"Yes and yes. It's an apartment, and I will need, you know, everything to set up a place I can call home."

"Of course you do. You look well, Annie. A new adventure agrees with you."

I offered her coffee or tea, and we went into the kitchen so I could prepare it.

"What's in the tote?"

"Annie, I found so much of Charlotte's belongings that my mother saved," she said breathlessly. "I didn't bring all of what I found, just what I thought could help us understand the letter from the Navy. I can't tell you how creepy that letter made me feel. You know, I always knew she was some sort of war hero, but this made it real for me."

"She must have been very brave," I said. "I am anxious to learn about her now. You're right, it makes her real. She's in our DNA, Mom."

Fumbling around in the tote, she produced a packet of letters tied with red, white and blue yarn.

"I want you and Randall, and J, and Ty to read these with me. Together we can piece the puzzle together."

"It's like visiting with her ghost, isn't it?" At this remark Mom started and dropped the letters.

# CHAPTER 5

## *Charlotte's Letters*

"What's the matter, Mom? You look like you've already seen a ghost."

"As I said, this experience has been a little creepy. I haven't been back to that house in years."

"What's the house like?" I asked. It was all news to me, this story about my family. I wanted to know whatever Mom could tell me. *An old house with an attic full of mystery. Right up my alley*, I thought.

"It's a beautiful house, Annie. My new tenants love it and have asked if they can research some restoration projects for me. It has a lovely entryway, a grand stairway and lots of nooks and crannies. You'll see it. We have to go back and get the rest of the stuff in the attic."

Mom paused, collecting herself and the letters, and launched into the story of Charlotte.

"I didn't know if you'd be interested in these things. We

haven't had much opportunity to talk." Mom's eyes cast down at the contents of the tote. She took a deep breath and caught a tear before it fell onto the letters. "Charlotte was engaged to a Navy pilot who flew the very plane she was testing and flying to California. She was both a test pilot for Grumman and a WASP. Well, her fiancé was killed in that plane, flying a mission in the Pacific. Not that exact plane, but that model, the Avenger."

I poured two cups of coffee and let the steam from the cup fill my nose. I was starting to wrap my mind around the ideas that this lady, Charlotte, was my ancestor.

"Are there any photos of them, Charlotte and what's his name?"

"I knew you would ask that. Let's take my stash into the living room where we can spread it out. I love old photographs." She smiled, a little pink flush rising in her cheeks. She rummaged through the red tote, sending up a cloud of old paper smell.

Trouble was awake now and wasted no time climbing up Mom's jeans leg to see what she had in her lap.

"She's very cute," Mom said, rubbing the itch out of the claw marks just planted in her leg.

"Ah, here!" She handed me a studio photo of a young man, maybe mid-twenties. He looked directly into the camera with eyes that could have been blue or green, maybe hazel. One corner of his mouth turned up and his head was cocked slightly to the right. He wore the white scarf and leather bomber jacket of a Navy pilot. A lock of dark hair fell onto his forehead from under his captain's hat. At the bottom of the photo, he had written, *We'll fly together. Love to Love, Frank.*

"Nice work, Great Gramma! What a hottie." I smiled up at Mom.

She handed me another. "This is Charlotte."

"God, Mom. You look just like her."

The photo reminded me of the ones you see in magazine articles about old movie stars. Charlotte looked at something slightly up and to her left. It made her blue eyes in this colored photo appear translucent. Her hair was very blond and floated softly around her head and shoulders. Her lips were slightly parted as if she had just been kissed. I wanted to find out everything I could about this lady. Not to mention her Frank.

"I feel like I want to know them. You have to tell me everything you remember or ever heard about them." I grew up with no aunts or uncles or cousins, so naturally I was starved for information about these new additions to my wispy family tree.

Like a magician pulling rabbits out of her hat, Mom produced another photo, a snapshot, black and white. Frank sat in the cockpit of a fighter plane while Charlotte stood on the ground looking up at him, her hand resting on the fuselage.

"Look at the side of the plane, Annie. Pilots liked to have a favorite cartoon figure like Bugs Bunny or a glamorous girl painted on the plane, with a message for the enemy."

"I see! It's a caricature of Charlotte." Below the decal

painted in script was the word, Char. I laid the photos on the small space on the coffee table not covered by my boxes.

"We need to preserve these," I said, and Mom nodded. She was warm and alive with the excitement of her discoveries. I could like this Mom.

"The letters, Mom?" I asked.

"Yes." She reached for the packet of letters and untied the yarn. "I want to see if you see the same thing I do, Annie."

"What do you mean?"

"I'm going to lay the letters out on the floor, side by side, and I want you to tell me what you see."

She knelt on the floor and handed me half the pack. "Here, help me. Chronology doesn't matter. They're all dated, and we can put them back in order later."

We laid the letters out like tiles on the floor. They were all written on light blue flimsy paper with red and blue striped edges.

"This paper is the air mail stationery everyone used during the war," Mom explained. "Okay, what do you see?"

"I don't know." Trouble had started her own inspection of the letters. Before she decided to make a cat's version of paper airplanes out of them, I plucked her off Mom's display.

"Let's see. They all start, *My Darling.* The format is the same. The messages are different, as are the lengths. Nothing unusual here. Oh, every one of them has a string of numbers at the bottom. Are they some sort of sign-off? No, they're all different." I started with the first letter, looking at each again, and then an idea hit me. "Hang on!"

I ran to the kitchen and returned with the copy of the note from the crashed plane. "Here, these sets of numbers are like the one at the bottom of the note the Navy found in the plane in Appalachia."

Mom took it. She cocked her head and looked at me. Waiting for the penny to drop she drawled, "Sooooooo?"

# CHAPTER 6

## *Code*

"I think it's a code." Mom's statement was firm. She looked really proud of herself.

"How can we be sure? And how can we crack it?" I had to agree with her conclusion.

"I have one more item from the trunk in the attic." Mom rummaged around in the tote again. Out came a dog-eared volume, <u>Latin I and II</u>, an old Latin textbook.

"I found one of the letters tucked in this book. Could it be one of those book based codes?"

"What do you mean?" This was a job for someone like my boyfriend, Ty. I know zip about codes. Except, of course, the DNA code I will be studying in my Bio classes.

Mom explained. "Well, with book codes, your numbers represent page numbers or word counts. You have to decide the rules for your code. Suppose you use the number 2. It could mean page 2, the second word on the page or . . ."

"Okay, I see! Is there anything in the Latin book to give away the key to their code?"

"I haven't found it yet. But I think you and Ty are the super sleuths in this family, so I wanted you to have first crack."

I chuckled at her pun.

The doorbell rang. I rose to get it, my knees cracking loudly. Peeking through the peephole, I could see Ty peeking back. Whenever Ty appeared, I felt like someone had turned up the electricity. Everything just lit up.

I let him in. He picked me up, no mean feat, and gave me a big bear hug, growling into my hair. It was such a lovely feeling to disappear into his tall muscular self.

"You smell like you just put gas in the car," I mumbled into his neck.

"That's a-v-i-a-t-i-o-n fuel!" He drew out the word, expecting a reaction.

"That's right! You were at the airfield today. How'd it go?"

"You have company, Annie?" Ty said, looking into the den.

Ty had never met my mother. "Shhh." I held my finger to my lips. "My mom's here." Ty's expression was priceless: eyebrows disappearing behind the dark hair that fell across his forehead, jaw dropping open, green eyes wide.

"Oh," he managed. "Is that good?" he whispered.

"You'll see. It's actually exciting."

Before I could lead Ty into the living room he scooped me back into his arms for a kiss. He took my left hand and gently twisted the ring on my finger. I twisted it back. It was the ring he had given me in Turkey. It represented our commitment to each other and every time we saw each other, we twisted the ring. Taking him by the hand, I introduced him to my mother.

"Mom, this is Tyler Egan. He's just come from the airfield and I think he may have a surprise for us."

Ty went over to Carol and shook her hand, saying he was pleased to finally meet her.

She blushed, saying, "Ty, tell us about your day at the airfield. We have a mystery here that has to do with planes as well."

"Let's hear your mystery first, because I am taking you ladies to dinner tonight! Is your dad around, Annie, and Aunt J?"

"You did it, didn't you?" I threw my arms in the air.

"Yup. I passed my solo."

"Hmmm. Another pilot in the family." Carol's eyes sparkled.

I looked at Mom and wondered what other surprises would spring from the red tote.

"Nice work Great Gramma! What a hottie." I smiled. "Mom,
the letters?" I asked. Yes. She pulled them out of her tote
and said, "I want to see if you see the same things I do."

# CHAPTER 7

## Generations

"Ty, you won't believe what Mom has been telling me about a mystery concerning my great-grandmother. Mom, this is your story, and maybe Ty can see something we don't. Can you fill him in on the details, so far? I'm just hearing this story for the first time, too."

"Well, let me start with . . ." She shuffled the papers in her lap. "Here's the letter we received from the Department of the Navy. And here's a copy of a note we found in the plane. The note is written on some sort of a company form with and identification number on it. The number belonged to Charlotte, my grandmother."

"I also have a letter from the Naval Crime Investigation Service about the condition of the plane where they found the note, and the pilot they found in the wreckage. There are skeletonized remains of a person whose identity they are trying to confirm. They know who flew the plane when it went missing, but they must confirm that it is that person. It is a woman."

Mom added a new thought, "You know, it's ironic. Charlotte did die in a plane crash many years later. She continued to fly recreationally after the war. When I went to Maryland to see if there was any record of her time at Grumman, I found these letters in the house where Charlotte spent her last years."

Ty crouched over the treasures and picked carefully through the letters, selecting one and then the next, handling each with care, his long fingers lingering over certain ones. His hair fell over his brow, creased with concentration, and I controlled the urge to tuck it back in place.

Trouble was sprawled across Ty's suede boots, purring loudly. In her demented kitty mind, she may think she's related to whatever beast the leather came from.

"All these strings of numbers are different, but six of them have the last five numbers the same. I bet they will help us find the key to the code," Ty said and looked up at us. He reached for the Latin textbook in Carol's lap. "What's this?"

"Mom thinks it's the key to the code."

"So it's up to us to crack it? What about the Navy? Isn't NCIS investigating all of this?"

Mom shook her head. "I don't want to give these personal letters to them just yet. I think we can find out a lot on our own. It's our family. This is my only link with my grandmother. I bet they can crack the code, but if we can, I might get a better sense of who she was, and what part she played in the war."

"And, Mom, why were she and her boyfriend writing in code? Could they have been spies, or even saboteurs?" These intriguing and unnerving thoughts occurred to me, and that could be why my mother was concerned.

Ty raked his fingers through the hair that had fallen in his eyes. "I have a couple of computer geek friends at school. They might see this as a sort of fun project," he offered. "But what do you say, Annie? Let's try first. It's your call, Ms. Wheeler."

"Yes. You two try first. I have complete faith in you both." She smiled at us. Her look of worry disappeared as the creases in her brow smoothed out. She really was very pretty. "It's settled then!" Mom excused herself and slipped into the powder room.

Changing the subject, I ventured, "Ty, when can I get a ride in the plane?"

"Whoa, what plane? The pilot's license doesn't come with a plane."

"Oh." I couldn't hide my disappointment. "I thought you could borrow one. You know, just pay for the fuel and away we go."

"It's possible my instructor would let us do that. Come to think of it, he mentioned that his father worked at a defense plant here on Long Island during WWII. I wonder if he can help us out with this mystery. Let me see if I can get Jazz to set up a meeting for us with his dad."

"Jazz?"

"Yeah. Jazz Wiedermeier. He's a VietNam vet. He was

a stunt pilot in air shows for a while and now runs the pilot training school at Republic Field."

"Would he like to take us up in his plane? We could loop the loop and all that Jazz."

# CHAPTER 8

## *What Evidence?*

Ty rolled his eyes at me, picked up the sleeping kitten, definitely her cutest time, and put her in her bed, hidden under an overturned box. She gave a loud purr and curled herself into a ball, paws covering her face. We grinned down at her like proud parents, our arms around each other.

"Are you taking her to Vermont?" Ty asked. "Or will you leave her with Aunt J?"

"Can you see this cat with Aunt J? Really? She goes with me."

Mom emerged from the bathroom and we left to celebrate Ty's pilot status.

"Aunt J and Dad are going to meet us at the restaurant." Ty had called ahead while we waited for Mom.

"Oh, nice," Mom replied with a fake smile on her face.

I guessed she had lost her place as the central focus of this mystery, now that everyone was in the mix. I didn't feel very good about thinking this way. Why was I so reluctant to give her a chance?

There are a lot of restaurants in Manhattan. Duh, what an understatement. We had a favorite on a side street down a flight of stairs below a Brownstone. In the old days, the entrance located at the bottom of the stairs was for the servants. It was simply called OUR KITCHEN. The menu included what you would cook at home, if you had the time: meat loaf, veggie lasagna, chili, beef stew, real comfort food.

The walls of the restaurant were natural brick and over the years, customers had left messages on them with chalk provided by the owners. The floors consisted of big slabs of stone with cement in between. The ceiling was the only new thing in the place. It was covered with those copper metal tiles with a design pressed into them. Round tables were covered with royal blue cloths. The chairs were like modern desk chairs, rollers and all.

Everyone arrived, hugs and greetings were exchanged, and we settled in to order our food and beverages. I peered over my menu and asked Dad what we needed to do next with the Navy's letter.

"The Navy is investigating under NCIS and processing the plane as if it were a crime scene. Civilian crashes are investigated by the National Transportation Safety Board, NTSB, but this was a military plane. The plane went down in good weather. They suspect some sort of mechanical failure. The fact that the plane was brand new and had been checked out before the flight makes this a real mystery."

"How can they check a plane that's so old?'

"There are a few engineers still kicking around. They are being brought in to inspect the wreckage, which is not in such bad shape. In addition, there are a lot of plane enthusiasts who have restored these planes for museums and the like. They are experts on how to make them work when they don't."

Jill put down her fork. "The identity of the pilot? How's that coming?"

"Female. They can tell from the skeleton. She's young. As you know the Grumman records reveal who was flying the plane when it went missing. It's a matter of confirming the records with the remains."

Absent-mindedly, I made designs in my mashed potatoes, little airplanes bumping into clouds. I was still trying to wrap my head around this amazing story, and that it had to do with my family. I listened, impressed with how much Aunt Jill and Dad knew about the details of an investigation like this one.

"Do those records exist?" I asked.

"I'm sure they do," Dad said.

Ty added, "I'm surprised that the skeleton was intact. Usually, remains that are out in the elements become targets for animals, eating them, scattering the bones, or, in the case of small rodents, using them for nest building. How come the remains are in such good condition?" Ty's question arose from his knowledge of what happens to human remains. He'd been working at an archaeological dig as part of his doctoral degree.

"According to some initial notes I saw, the flight suit, goggles, helmet and boots were made of tough enough fabric and leather to prevent what you just described," Dad said.

"How will they identify her?" This was the main question for me.

"Her personal effects, the clothing, dental records," Aunt J supplied.

"That's the thing. There were no personal effects, no purse, nothing in the pockets, just the signature on the roster."

"What about DNA?"

"That technology wasn't available back then. Samples of DNA were not taken from personnel involved in military activities the way they are today."

"But what if they get a tentative ID? Can't they match DNA from her hair or bones to that of a living relative?"

"Way to go, Annie," Ty said. "But they have to get that tentative ID."

"Why was there a note in the crashed plane for great gramma's fiancé? How did she know it would get to him?" I asked.

"We don't know if it was for Charlotte's fiancé. It could have been for any pilot," Mom said.

"There is a lot for us to find out," I said.

"Too bad we can't time travel, Annie," Mom said.

"Maybe we can," Ty said with a wink. "Are you up for a trip to the airport tomorrow?"

The waiter brought our food and drinks and we toasted Ty's new pilot's license. I looped my leg around his, smiling around my meat loaf. "I cannot wait to have my first flight with you! What's the plane like?

# CHAPTER 9

## *All That Jazz*

The airport in Farmingdale, Long Island was where Ty had trained for his pilot's license, and where his flight instructor would arrange for us to meet his father, a contemporary of my great-grandmother.

We left Aunt J's Manhattan apartment at 5:30AM to beat the traffic.

"You drive, Annie. Don't want you to get rusty. When was the last time you drove a Jeep with a stick shift?"

"You're right. I should drive," I said, inwardly chuckling. "I haven't driven since our time in Turkey."

Traffic was blessedly light, and soon we pulled off the Long Island Expressway, heading for Farmingdale. The local road, which was crowded with malls and stores, suddenly opened up to a wide expanse of space. A long runway ended behind a fence at the edge of the road. The control tower was visible in the distance. A sign pointed to the entrance and I turned, taking the driveway to an area with several hangars.

Ty pointed, "This field was part of the old Republic Aviation plant. They made airplanes just like Grumman did, the company your great-grandmother worked for."

"What are all those abandoned buildings? They're huge."

"Those are the old plane factories."

"Obviously they don't make planes anymore," I said.

"The company went out of business. This is a commercial airport now."

"You just can't get away from the whole aviation thing on L.I., can you?" I said.

"Nope. Long Island is known as the Cradle of Aviation. The Wright Brothers got off the ground in Kitty Hawk, North Carolina, but the big advances in aviation happened here."

"Didn't Charles Lindbergh take off from a field near here for his famous flight to Paris?"

"Yup. The first non-stop trans-Atlantic flight took off from Roosevelt Field. It's a big shopping mall now with a lot of commemorative plaques and artwork."

We pulled into the parking lot and headed toward a building with a sign advertising Republic Field Flying School.

"Thanks for letting me drive," I said.

Ty grinned and grabbed a back pack from the back seat of the Jeep. "Glad to see you haven't lost your touch. C'mon,

Annie, let's check out the plane. I'll show you the safety check list that a pilot does before takeoff."

Ty was absolutely on fire with his new love, flying. I wondered if I should be jealous.

"Don't the mechanics here do all that?" I think even if they did, Ty would want to do his own checking. More time with the plane.

"No. If you fly the plane, you want to do your own checkout. If the plane gets into trouble, it doesn't help to blame it on someone else."

"Makes sense. What do you want me to do?"

"Just watch me. I'll go through the list, and you make sure I cover all the items. Here's a pen."

"Okay, but this looks complicated."

"It is, but you need to learn it if you want to fly with me. It's a safety issue. What if I became disabled during a flight?"

I felt sweat popping out all over at Ty's question. "Does the plane come with parachutes?"

"Annie, if you take care of business, flying is safer than driving. Besides, it's a Federal Aviation Administration regulation."

"Yeah, I've heard that on the news reports when the National Transportation Safety Board gets involved in investigations of plane crashes."

"Help me take the tarp off the windscreen."

As I grabbed one side of the tarp, I remembered the time Ty and I spent sailing around Fire Island. We met there and besides investigating a very active ghost, he taught me how to sail. Ty walked around the plane, checking moveable sections of its wings and tail, the propeller, the tires and some mechanism involved with the landing gear. He called out, "*Landing gear position lights*," and then, "*Flight controls*."

As I went through this routine with Ty, I imagined Charlotte doing the same before she took off back in the 1940's. I'd been thinking about her a lot since Mom and Dad told me about the letter from the Navy. I feel like she was finding a home in my brain. *Brrr. That gave me a chill.*

"Be right back." Ty broke the spell as he headed toward the hangar.

"Okay," I called after him, and turned back to the plane.

*I wonder how you get inside.*

I leaned closer, to see how I could reach the door to the cockpit. It was over the wing. *Can you step on the wing? Will it break if I do?*

I looked down at the wing. *Well, look at that. It said STEP HERE right on the wing surface under the door.* A series of nonskid treads led right to the door.

A quick look in the direction of the hangar offered no clue as to where Ty had gone, so up I went. The door was unlocked. I went into the cockpit and slid down into the seat behind the controls. An image of Charlotte in the cockpit of the Avenger came unbidden.

*Lost in her own thoughts about what she had found, Charlotte failed to notice a figure hidden in the shadows, watching her.*

# CHAPTER 10

## *What Charlotte Saw*

1943

*Charlotte Wheeler was about to* finish her twelve hour shift. She and her crew had just put the finishing touches on Avenger #1022. Most of the team had a big stake in making sure the planes left the plant in perfect condition. This Avenger was headed to the Pacific to help win the war. The survival of America, democracy, and so many husbands, fathers, brothers, and sweethearts was on the line.

Charlotte's fiancé, Frank Bradenton, was a pilot, specifically an Avenger pilot. Charlotte thought of these last checks as a special prayer to keep Frank safe, like crossing your fingers behind your back.

Her workspace was a mighty cavern. It was two football fields long, three to four stories tall, and filled with planes in all stages of construction. Light streamed in during the day from the high windows. *Traveling cranes hung from beams. Large grappling hooks that positioned the heavy plane parts, like engines or wings, dangled across the wide space. Crates with names like Pratt and Whitney, General Electric, and Sperry were piled next to the unfinished planes. Tools of every kind were stashed in huge red rolling cases and power tools like rivet guns hung from electric cables.*

*Charlotte smiled a little at the rivet guns. You couldn't hear yourself think here in the plant because the guns never stopped. In fact, they would start up again in a few minutes, as the plant shifts continued twenty-four/seven. The women who worked those guns were affectionately known as "Rosie the Riveter". WE CAN DO IT, proclaimed a poster pasted to the side of a traveling ladder. It featured a pretty woman in the ever-present blue coveralls and red bandana, flexing her bicep.*

*Charlotte's heart raced as she approached the newly finished plane. She climbed the ladder and stepped off onto the wing, swinging one leg and then the other onto the pilot's seat, sliding down to sit in it.*

*She had flown Avengers to California many times and knew the pilots' checklist. She flipped a switch on the control panel and engaged electrical power, looking at the gauges and controls.*

*There were thirty items to review including the obvious ones, altimeter and fuel gauge. Other dials and indicators showed the pilot how the engine was performing and how to manipulate fuel mixture. Controls for the aircraft during takeoff, flight and landing, especially on the deck of an aircraft carrier, were not really* gauges but handles, levers and bars. There were indicators for the bomb bays, and controls for the bomb bay doors.

Charlotte checked every last one. Everything worked. Then she went back for what she called her special "Here's you, Frank" check, and did it all again. It wasn't easy having a fiancé who flew the same plane you built and flew. This time, the bomb bay door release felt loose in her hand. There was no snapping noise to indicate that it was engaged to the mechanism that opened the doors. Charlotte's stomach did a queasy flip. This had to be reported!

She slipped out of the cockpit to the cement floor. Fishing in the back pocket of her dark blue overalls for the form used to report a malfunction, Charlotte realized she had forgotten to leave her note for the pilot, a ritual she performed for every plane, secretly hoping the pilot would be, by some miracle, Frank.

Quick as a bunny, she climbed back onto the wing and, balancing on her stomach, stashed the note in a place where the pilot would find it. Back on the floor, she kissed her fingertips and touched the plane's fuselage just under the cockpit. She pulled off her bandana and headed for the hangar exit. Lost in her own thoughts about the bomb bay door lever, she failed to notice the figure hidden in the shadows. It lingered, watching her retreating figure in those blue overalls, blonde hair swinging, twirling her bandana as she hurried away.

# CHAPTER 11

## *A Witness to History*

Ty was back, breaking into my daydreams about what Charlotte Wheeler's life was like. A small wiry man with frizzy gray hair that was balding on top and sporting a ponytail, was slapping Ty on the back.

"Congratulations, kiddo. You did it."

"You're going to have to tell me everything I need to know about this Piper Cherokee."

"You bet. We got time, pal."

I climbed out of the cockpit. Both guys looked at me as if I were the genie just out of the proverbial bottle. "I was looking at the instrument panel to see what I could find on the pilot's checklist," I explained.

"This is Annie Tillery, my girl. Annie, Mr. Jazz Wiedermeier."

"Just Jazz is fine. How did you get into the cockpit?"

Jazz looked me over with his pale blue eyes. His sharp tone

bordered on unfriendly. *What was the problem with my getting into the cockpit?*

"I climbed onto the wing where it said STEP HERE, opened the door, and got in. Ty was showing me the pilot's checklist, and I was checking."

Ty looked surprised by Jazz's harsh question.

"Is there a problem?" we asked in unison.

"No, no. Sorry. Just touchy about someone I don't know getting into the plane. 9/11, you know." He jammed his hands into his pockets, grinning with a shake of his head. Abruptly, he turned to Ty and explained the steps he required to release the plane from the cables that were holding it down.

"Jazz?" I interrupted their conversation. It seemed they'd never finish discussing the various nuts and bolts of the Cherokee.

"Jazz!" I said a little louder. Both of them turned around.

"I need to ask you a favor."

"Sure, the ladies' room is . . ."

"No. Not that." *Really,* I thought.

"Okay, shoot."

"I just found out . . ." I stopped. "Did Ty tell you about my great-grandmother, and her time at Grumman?"

"Some."

"I wonder if I could talk to your dad. Ty says he worked on planes during the war. Do you think he would talk to me? It sure would help me get a better picture of her story."

Jazz slid his cell from his back pocket and tapped a button. "Dad? Jazz."

Jazz's eyes twinkled. "I have a young lady here who would love to speak to you about the good old days." After a pause, Jazz's eyes lit up again. "Yes, she is very pretty." He smiled at me. "Can she come now?" Jazz looked at me.

I nodded. *Great luck!* I thought.

"Okay, Dad. Fifteen minutes."

"Let's go." Ty said and gave a last cursory tug to the tarp he had replaced on the plane and we headed toward Jazz's red Mustang. "We'll have to check out the plane later."

# CHAPTER 12

## *Mr. Wiedermeier's Virtual Flying Lesson*

We drove the short distance to Mr. Wiedermeier's home in Old Bethpage.

"Isn't Bethpage where the Grumman plant is?" This didn't look like a factory town to me.

"Yup. Not too far away from here," Jazz said, leading us up a brick walk to the back door.

Old Mr. Wiedermeier was standing at the door with a cup of tea.

"Dad just turned ninety-six," Jazz said.

"Gosh, Mr. Wiedermeier, you don't look a day over eighty," I gasped, wondering whether I had just insulted him.

"What's your name, young lady? I like you. And if I were eighty, I'd ask you for a date. Call me Felix."

I giggled. "I like you, too."

Mr. Wiedermeier, I mean Felix, must have been quite the guy in his day. He was a nice looking gentleman. He was only average height with a slim build, but he stood straight as an arrow which made him look taller. His features were fine, the skin on his face, stretched like parchment, revealing tiny lines but few wrinkles. His cheeks were rosy, eyes a darker blue than his son's.

He led us into a kitchen where a scarred and stained pine table was set with tea cups and a plate of cookies, maybe even homemade.

"Snickerdoodles. I make 'em myself." He smiled proudly at the plate. "Please sit. I'll play mother and pour the tea. My wife passed last year," he said softly.

"I'm so sorry," I murmured. Ty nodded.

He filled our cups and I took a cookie, controlling the urge to take six. I was starving.

"So your great-grandmother worked for Grumman?"

"Yes, on the Avenger. I wonder if you could tell me anything about what it was like to build planes during war time."

"Well, let's see. I worked in the plant because I couldn't get into the armed services. Bad ticker," he said patting his chest. He looked up and winked, "Fooled 'em, didn't I?"

"You sure did." I smiled. "Tell us about your job."

"I worked at Grumman on the Avenger, like you great-gramma. What was her name?"

"Charlotte. Charlotte Wheeler."

Felix frowned and paused, as if trying to pluck something from those memories of his job at Grumman.

"Tell us about the Avenger. I know some things, but I'd like to hear about it from someone who was there. What was it like? It's so overwhelming to think of every person in the country involved in winning that war."

"Well, my job was to dispatch the finished planes to California. They were making ten planes a day between 1942 and 1945, ten thousand in total, so I didn't sit around much. They used to call me Sarge."

"Were you there when a plane went missing? I think it was, like, around, June 1943."

"How do you know about that?" Felix's response was sharp.

I explained about the letter my mother had received, out-lining how they traced the note to Charlotte. "It was in the wreckage, on Charlotte's repair form."

Felix frowned and looked down at his tea, then put the cup down, a slight tremor in his hand. "Brenda McPhee. I sent her off. The plane checked out. The weather was clear. I don't know what could have happened."

At the mention of Brenda's name, I gasped. "You have to contact the Navy, Mr. Wiedermeier. They are trying to verify the identity of the remains in the plane. You could be so helpful."

"I will. I just didn't know." He seemed very unsettled, not knowing what to do.

"My mom should be getting some information from the Naval Criminal Investigation Service soon. It should tell us what, if anything, they found."

Jazz added, "You know most plane crashes are due to pilot error."

Felix gave Jazz a penetrating look.

I persisted. "Do you remember anything at all about problems with the planes, or reported sabotage?"

At the word *sabotage*, Felix Wiedermeier's head snapped up.

"No, no, nothing at all. In fact, I don't remember any more than I've told you. I think I have to take a rest now, if you don't mind." He got up from the table abruptly and left the room.

I looked at Ty, whose face showed bewilderment. Jazz, however, was tight-lipped, offering no explanation or apology. His chair scraped loudly as he got up. "Let me take you back to the field."

"Is your dad okay? Did I upset him?"

"No, he's just old. Sometimes he talks a blue streak about his war time experiences. Maybe it's losing that girl in the plane crash."

*Maybe he knew there was something wrong with the plane,* I thought.

# CHAPTER 13

## Clues in the Code

"Ty, we never got to fly."

I was disappointed, no airplane ride, and no real information from Mr. Wiedermeier. And we still didn't know what those numbers in Charlotte's and Frank's letters meant. If we could just figure out the code, I felt we could find out what happened back in Charlotte's 1943.

As if reading my mind, Ty said, "Why don't we try to break the code in those letters?"

"How did you know what I was thinking?" I punched his arm playfully as we climbed back into the Jeep to return to New York City. We got to Aunt J's apartment in time for dinner. The aroma of something delicious enveloped us in its mouthwatering heaven.

Before we could get our coats off, Aunt J appeared, carrying a steaming platter that looked like it could feed an army.

"I heard the elevator," she said and placed the food on the

dining room table. "It's rosemary chicken with wild mushrooms and baby potatoes. Annie, get drinks for everyone. Ty, slice the bread. Wash your hands."

"Yes, Ma'am," we saluted.

"We are going to work on the code in the letters after dinner, Aunt Jill," I said as we dug into the delicious food. "Want to help?"

"Sure. Have some more chicken," she urged.

As always, Aunt J cooked, and the cleanup was left to Ty and me. I went to the kitchen and opened the hot water tap to fill the sink, added dish soap and watched a mountain of opalescent bubbles form. "I am going to miss her so much," I said, poking at the bubbles.

"And her cooking," he added.

Aunt J came into the kitchen and opened a bottle of red wine. Filling her glass, she waved the bottle at Ty, who shook his head. "Water's fine, Aunt J."

I wasn't legally old enough to drink and J obeyed the law, even at home.

We made short work of the washing, and left the dishes to air dry, because the letters were calling to us. I collected them from my desk and we spread them out on the dining room table.

Aunt J joined us from the den where she had been relaxing with her glass of wine. "Okay, let's do this like the real detectives we are. We can start with some basic questions. What do they all have in common? Don't leave anything out, not even the most obvious detail."

"The type of stationery," I said.

"And the confounded string of numbers," Ty said. He was thumbing through the <u>Latin I and II</u> textbook my mother had found with the letters.

"Hey, look. There's something else. All around the border of each letter is the phrase 'I love you' in several languages."

I held one of the letters up to the light. "You know, these *I love you*'s are handwritten, not printed on the paper. At first, I thought they were some cutesy border created by the stationery company."

"But it's so carefully done, it looks like part of the stationery," Jill added.

Ty continued to fan the pages of the Latin text. "Look, there's an almost imperceptible gap between pages in a few locations here."

"The Latin word for love is *amo?*" Ty said, shuffling through the Latin text.

"*Amo, amas, amat,*" I recited, rolling my eyes at the memory of my high school Latin course.

"Don't knock it, Annie. You will be very happy you learned Latin when you have to learn all those biological and medical terms." Ty continued. "Just a hunch, but I'm going to see if any of the forms of the verb, *to love*, appear on any of the pages, on either side of these gaps. Books have sort of a muscle memory when you use certain pages over and over again."

We looked at the first page that stood out in the book's muscle memory. "Yahoo, the first word on the page is *amo*!" I said, ruffling Ty's hair.

There were ten pages that bracketed Ty's "gaps." Eight of them had one of the Latin forms of *to love* as the first word on the page.

"And look, there is a tiny dot at the bottom of each page, almost hidden in the spine." Ty showed us what he had found.

"So, now what?" Aunt J was looking at one of the letters and chewing on her knuckles, a sure sign she was wrestling with the code. "I have an idea. What are the numbers of the pages starting with *amo?*"

I listed the numbers. "3, 20, 48, 67, 71, 83, 91 and 103."

"Now, look at the letters," she instructed. "Look at the string of numbers." She grabbed a pad of sticky notes from the telephone table and placed a column of the little green squares on the dining room table, each labeled with one of the page numbers I had just recited.

Ty and I sorted the letters, placing each next to the appropriate sticky note. Four letters did not fit with any page number.

Ty smacked his forehead. "I get it, Aunt J! Let's try using the rest of the numbers in the string to count out the words on the page."

For page 3, we took the first number and counted out the corresponding word in the text which was *the*. That was encouraging. The rest of the numbers corresponded with words that made no sense, and we ran out of words before we ran out of numbers.

"What if we count the letters on the page, not the words?" Jill offered.

She counted and called out letters. I wrote them down. I held up what I had written. My heart was pounding.

SABOTAGE WHAT CAN WE DO

"Oh, God," Jill said. "Is that why the plane crashed?"

"Did they stop the sabotage?" I said. "This opens a Pandora's box of so many questions."

"It sure does," Aunt J agreed. "Was this Charlotte's and Frank's secret alone?

"And, how do we find answers?" We looked at each other, wondering what to do next.

"Maybe, we can find out if we Google, *Sabotage on the Avenger.*" Ty reached in his pocket for his smart phone.

"I don't know if you'll find anything, Ty," Jill said. "That would have been top secret. You might get somewhere with the Department of the Navy."

"Maybe Dad can help us. He has in the past. He has a lot of connections."

"We don't know what this means. It could refer to something else. We need to decode the other messages." Aunt J's logic, as always, was spot on.

A memory of Felix Wiedermeier's strange behavior nagged at me. He worked at that plant. I couldn't help feeling he was hiding something.

The phone rang. Aunt J handed it to me. "It's your mom."

Mom, I was sure, would either clear things up or make them more complicated. I listened, telling Mom we would make arrangements and get back to her. Ty and Aunt J looked on like two collies waiting for the command to go after some lost sheep.

"NCIS has the forensics report on the plane crash in the Appalachians. Mom's taking the Amtrak to Washington, D.C. She wants me to come. She'll check to see if they know anything about Charlotte."

"Let's fly down to Washington, Annie. We can take the Cherokee. I need to log the hours."

"You are so on!" I jumped up and planted a big kiss on Ty's lips with an equally big hug.

"What about the rest of these letters?" J asked.

"We'll have to work on them when we come back," I said.

"I won't touch them. I think we're on to something. Wish I could go with you, but I have this thing called a job."

She looked at Ty. "You do know how to fly that little Cherokee, don't you? Take care, both of you."

# CHAPTER 14

## Committing It to Paper

1943

*Shaking uncontrollably, Charlotte needed to* talk to someone *she trusted about the bomb bay door lever. She had checked some of the other planes and about half had the same problem. She had instructed the woman in charge of each plane to replace the lever, explaining that a defect was suspected.*

*Should she report what she had found? If it was sabotage, was it an inside job? That would make catching the saboteurs more difficult. To whom could she report what she had found? For now, until she could get Frank's opinion, she decided to check each plane herself before it went out.*

*How to tell Frank? She pulled out her stationery box and began to write to him, but stopped. Mail was censored because of spies and sabotage. At the bottom of the box was an old Latin textbook. She knew why it was in her stationery box. She and Frank,* teenage sweethearts, had written coded letters to each other in high school. She remembered the code and how very secret it was.

Charlotte scooped up her stationery and the Latin text and headed for her car. She hated to use the gasoline, so precious because it was rationed. She drove to the end of Woodcleft Canal in Freeport, a favorite secluded spot where she and Frank went to be alone. Charlotte could almost feel his presence as she began to write her first coded letter to her sweetheart.

# CHAPTER 15

## *Spy Land*

Jazz helped us remove the windshield tarp and release the cables that held the plane in place. Ty completed his checklist of the exterior of the plane. We got into the cockpit and he began to check the instrument panel, explaining as he went along. I was so excited. This was my first flight in a small plane, and this plane was really small. It was called a Piper Cherokee Arrow. Even the name gave me a little thrill.

"This plane was built in 1979," Ty said.

"Isn't it too old to fly?"

"Not if it's been properly maintained," Ty said, snapping his checklist log closed. He turned on the electrical system and checked a few more gauges. Out on the tarmac, Jazz gave us a thumbs up.

"Put on the headset, Annie. It'll be too noisy to talk when I turn on the engine, and you can listen to the tower talking to us."

I donned the headset and Ty reached over to turn it on. He showed me how to adjust the volume. "Belt up, my Annie. We are almost ready."

If it weren't for the belt, I would be floating around the plane. Glad I went to the bathroom before we started.

"Piper Cherokee N174CW prepared to taxi."

"Where are you headed, Piper N174CW?" came the tinny voice from the tower.

"Carroll County Regional Airport in Maryland. You should have my flight plan there."

"Roger that," the voice buzzed again. "You are cleared to taxi to runway two."

Ty revved the engine to full power, brakes on tight. He brought the engine down a few notches and eased off the brake. The little Cherokee moved into a lane heading for the runway, Ty steering with the rudders. He pointed at a wind sock.

"That cone-shaped thing shows wind direction."

I could see that we would be taking off into the wind, which allows the plane maximum lift. Ty spoke into the headset. "These little planes are made to fly, just like the little birds that inspired their design. In a stiff wind, it's hard to keep them on the ground."

The tower man spoke again. "When you line up with the runway, at my signal, you're good to go. Safe flight. And give that honey in the seat next to you a kiss for me."

"Will do."

I was giggling like a fool at this point, gripping my seat as tightly as I could. My face hurt from smiling.

"Clear."

Ty revved the engine full, took his foot off the brakes, raised the flaps and we raced down the runway, bouncing on the rough spots. Just when I thought we'd run out of runway, the bouncing stopped, the ground fell away and Ty banked the plane to take us to Maryland.

The wind was out of the west. We had to head east and then south to follow our flight plan from one vector to the next until we reached our destination. We gained altitude, all the while banking to gain our proper compass heading. Each banking maneuver gave me a sensation like falling in a tilting elevator. The instrument panel in front of me, just a jumble of dials yesterday, came alive for me. I could read our altitude and compass heading, how much fuel we had and whether this cool little plane was flying level.

Ty was busy checking other dials that had something to do with the engine. He fiddled with some levers until he was satisfied. Our speed was 125 miles per hour, but it seemed like we were just floating leisurely along, occasionally bumping into a cloud.

"How ya doin'?" Ty's voice crackled through my headset.

"It's way more cool than I could have imagined," I grinned. Even the idea that the thin plexiglass windscreen and side windows were all that kept us from being blown out of the plane, from falling five thousand feet to the ground, didn't take one tiny bit of joy out of this.

"Wow, Ty. I can't believe it's just you, me and the plane." *How much more romantic could this be?* I marveled.

"Would you like to take the controls for a bit?"

"What? Me? I, I . . . don't."

"Don't be a wuss. Just watch the wheel in front of you. This plane has dual controls. Can you see it move as I adjust the plane?"

I nodded.

"Okay, you can't make a mistake, because I can just take over if you send us into a dive. It's not like when we were in Turkey and had to change places in the Jeep while going sixty miles an hour."

"Yeah. That was one of our better tricks, don't you think?" I gave him a little poke on the arm. He kissed his fingers, and touched them to my mouth. My stomach did its little flip. This was so special.

"I love flying, being separated from the ground below, up here all alone. There's nothing like it," Ty said.

I looked out the window, watching the coast of New Jersey slip by. In a short while, Ty checked in with ground control in southern Jersey as we had entered a new vector. We banked again, turning inland over farms and small towns. The clouds grew a little thicker and Ty flipped the windshield wipers on as we flew through a cloud, shaking off some of its moisture.

"Neat way to wash the plane." Ty checked the compass

heading with his flight plan. "We'll be approaching the airport near New Windsor in Maryland very soon, Annie."

"This is the town where my mother grew up. The whole family lived here. I should come back with Mom some time. By the way, Ty, you do know how to land the plane, too, don't you?"

"Well I guess we'll see, won't we?" he joked back at me.

The engine started to make sputtering sounds. Ty stared at the instruments and started to move some of the levers. The engine choked again. Beads of sweat sprung out on his forehead.

"Annie, call Jazz. He's on my speed dial."

I don't know how I managed to connect to Jazz, my hands were shaking so badly.

Ty yelled, "Jazz, the engine's choking. Any ideas?" Ty looked hopefully at the phone and then at me. Our eyes locked on each other as we waited for Jazz.

"Give it full throttle. If there is something in the gas line, that should clear it," Jazz's voice crackled through the earphones.

Ty did it. The engine continued to miss. "No dice, Jazz."

"Do it again!"

Ty did it two more times and the engine noise evened out.

Ty wiped the sweat off his forehead. "What the hell was that all about?"

"Sometimes a little water gets in the gas line from condensation in the tank and it freezes at altitude. You just have to clear it, like you just did. But you're not high enough for freezing. Change all the fuel when you get to Maryland. If anything else happens, call. I'll be on standby. Use the radio."

We flew in silence for a while as Ty's full attention was on the instruments. After fifteen minutes, Ty said, "Okay, I think it's alright now. We're very close to Carroll County Airport anyway."

*But we're not very close to the ground,* I thought. Instead, I said, "You did good, Ty. I was scared." He reached over and took my hand. We held on tight for a while. We'd been through other scary stuff before, but not at this altitude.

Changing the subject, I said, "How are we getting to D.C. from this field, and why couldn't we land closer to the city, at Reagan or Dulles Airports?"

"Landing at major airports is a hassle for a small plane. And flying a small plane near D.C. requires security clearance. I called the manager at the airport. We can get a cab to the closest town, Westminster, and rent a car."

Ty radioed the tower at Carroll County Airport for information about wind direction, visibility, precipitation and runway conditions. We were cleared to land. The plane lost altitude and Ty slowed our speed as he leveled out, lining up with the runway. The ground began to rush up. Objects on the ground assumed their normal size as we kissed the ground. Ty braked and we taxied over to the main building, a combination hangar and office.

A man of about forty in mechanic's overalls came to meet

us. He yelled, "Park it over there. I'll take care of her. When'll ya be back?"

Ty answered and paid the airport fee. "We had a little problem with the fuel. Can you drain what's in there and give us a new load?"

"Sure, and I'll check 'er out for ya."

"Thanks."

"I called ya a taxi. Over there." He pointed and, waving, we got into the cab that was nothing like the yellow taxis in New York City. The driver took us through the rolling hills of Maryland to Westminster, where we rented an SUV . I set the GPS for NCIS headquarters in Quantico, Virginia. Robot-woman directed us to I-695, and we were on our way.

# CHAPTER 16

## Brenda McPhee

NCIS headquarters was in a big government complex. All the shields of the armed services' intelligence divisions were represented on the building's façade, giving the impression of military order and efficiency. It was intimidating, but reassuring at the same time. If anybody could find answers, it would be someone in this bee hive of modern technology.

Mom was waiting in the lobby, holding a file folder and looking nervously at the clock. We rushed up to her and took her arm. She hugged us both and her shoulders relaxed. "I'm so glad you're here. I was afraid something happened."

*Think I'll spare her the details of our little engine flutter.*

She fished in her folder and pulled out a paper. "I have to present this to the receptionist," she said. "It will get us into our appointment with the forensic pathologist."

*Better known as the "Doctor of the Dead",* I thought. I kept that to myself, too.

The receptionist accepted the letter. "Yes, Ma'am," she said and picked up the phone.

"If you wait just over there," she pointed to a group of sofas, "Someone will come for you."

We'd barely sat down when that someone arrived, a woman wearing a crisp white lab coat over scrubs.

"I'm Doctor Gianelli." She offered a hand to my mother. "Let me take you down to the lab. I've got my reports and test findings on the computer. You're Carol Wheeler, yes?"

"Yes, I am. And this is my daughter, Anne Tillery and her friend, Tyler Egan."

"We need to go to the basement level. That's where the forensics labs and the medical examiner's office are."

*Just like on TV. The labs and the medical examiner are always in the basement.* Another comment I'll keep to myself.

The elevator opened to a long brightly lit corridor with a tile floor, tiled walls, and stainless steel doors with wire mesh-reinforced windows. *Those TV shows sure do get it right.*

She opened the door and we filed in. I looked around at the various pieces of equipment. I had visited the forensics lab used by the New York City Police Department and remembered what a lot of this high tech stuff was.

A gas chromatography- mass spectrometer took up one corner of the room. This instrument could identify chemical compounds with the same degree of certainty as a fingerprint could be matched to one person. An electron microscope, used to identify and match hairs and fibers took up its own glassed-in space. There were gel boxes for electrophoresis used in protein and DNA analysis, centrifuges and hot plates. The room seemed to have all the same equipment I'd seen in the lab in New York.

Dr. Gianelli introduced us to Dr. Moriarty, and left. *Hmmm, Dr. Moriarty was Sherlock Holmes' nemesis,* I chuckled to myself.

"We do everything here, with the exception of ballistics, auto paint and fingerprints. Those go through the FBI lab," Dr. Moriarty said. "Let's take a look here. Now this is considered a cold case, because it's so old, but we treat every case with the same thoroughness. I'll sum up the basic findings for you. I'll give you the reports and you can have your own forensics expert go over them with you. Everything, including the pictures I'll show you on my computer, is in the report."

Dr. Moriarty cleared his throat and scratched his beard. "First, the plane. We found no mechanical failure, no evidence of the plane going down because of enemy fire. The fuel had evaporated, but there was residue in the tanks. That's still being analyzed. We should have the results in a few days. It appears the pilot, Brenda McPhee, was trying to land the plane, but overshot a small valley, crashing into a low cliff."

The good doctor pushed his glasses farther up his nose and flipped to another page. "The body, as analyzed by the forensic anthropologist, showed a massive fracture of the frontal bones of the cranium, caused by hitting the instrument panel. The windscreen was intact and her clothing allowed for a fair amount of preservation. There was some mummification of protected skin and organs. Some congealed blood was found inside her jacket and on her scarf."

"Wouldn't the blood be too old to be of any use?" Mom asked.

"No, Ma'am. We can type the blood of Egyptian mummies, amazingly enough. It depends on the way it's preserved. We were able to get her blood type in this case."

Dr. Moriarty continued, "Chemical analysis of her hair will tell us if any drug use was involved. I say her, not because of the Grumman record of McPhee being the pilot, but because the X-rays of the skeleton revealed the U-shaped pelvic symphysis, telling us the sex. The blood was well preserved and will give us DNA."

Brenda McPhee was a real person. Her young life was cut short in this accident. She was probably a friend of Charlotte's. An overwhelming sense of sadness washed over me and I reached for Ty's hand.

"How can you match her DNA to anything? There were no DNA data bases then," Ty asked.

"Since we have her dental records and Grumman records, we can trace her to living relatives and compare her DNA to the samples they provide." Dr. Moriarty closed the report and looked at us. "The basic story here is that the pilot, one Brenda McPhee, was flying a plane, a Grumman Avenger, newly manufactured at the plant in Bethpage, Long Island, to Miramar Naval/Air Base in California. The plane crashed in

Tennessee. It was discovered in October, 2014 by employees of a mining company."

"Was the plane ever reported missing?" I asked.

"Of course, Miss Tillery. I did tell you that it is a cold case, having been reported immediately when it failed to show up at Miramar. When a valuable military plane goes missing during wartime, you better believe there is an investigation. Now that we've identified the plane and pilot, we will try to find out why it crashed, though no apparent evidence points to a cause."

"Could it be sabotage?" Ty asked.

"It *was* wartime. We would love to know that, even if it happened seventy plus years ago. We can learn from every investigation and every crime."

We thanked Dr. Moriarty, who handed us his reports in a large manila envelope, shook our hands and left.

"How very sad for poor Brenda," Mom said, echoing my feelings.

"I've got to get the plane back today. Stay with your mom and see what else is in that attic," Ty said.

"Will you be okay flying alone?" I asked.

"Sure. Don't worry. Go with your mom. Something else might turn up. Attics are known for their secrets." Ty winked at me.

We kissed goodbye and went our separate ways.

"I like Ty," Mom said.

"Me, too," I replied, crossing my fingers for his safe return.

# CHAPTER 17

## Gramma Wheeler's Attic

"Here it is," Mom announced. We turned into a gravel drive-way that supported a fair amount of weeds. The house was set far back from the road, overlooking an expansive lawn uncluttered by trees and shrubs. The air was heavily scented with the latest mowing, definitely a smell I associated with the country.

The mowers, presumably the tenants, had left a wide border of lawn along the road to grow naturally. It was planted with colorful wildflowers.

The house was painted white with green shutters and a black door. It had that look of homey permanence, like your grandmother settling into the couch for a long visit.

Mom broke the silence. "New Windsor's really a cute little town, Annie."

"I thought so, too, Mom, when I drove through with Ty.

"Right. I forgot." As usual, Mom seemed embarrassed to have forgotten some fact or other.

"It's great to be here with you, though, Mom. You can tell me what it was like to grow up here."

"I loved living here. I was born in this house. And I almost remember Charlotte. I was only five when she died in that small plane crash. My mother lived here until she had to go to a nursing home. I wish I could have come back to take care of her."

Mom looked as if she were going to cry. I guess she felt guilty about not being able to take care of her mother, due to her own drinking, forcing her to go in and out of rehab. I knew it was time to change the subject.

"What did you like best about living here?"

"Oh, wait till you see the house." She sat up straighter, brightening at the prospect of telling me about her life in New Windsor.

We walked up a red brick path to the side door and rang the bell.

"The tenants are a young couple. Reminds me of you and Ty. She's pregnant with her first child. He works for the Internal Revenue Service in D.C.

*They're married and expecting their first child,* I thought. *And this reminds Mom of me and Ty?* I decided that my mother was losing her mind.

"How do you know all this?"

"I own the house, Annie, and I handled the rental."

"Oh, right," I muttered. *Maybe she's not such a busy body.*

There was no answer, and no cars in the driveway. "Guess no one's at home," I said.

"I have a key," Mom said fumbling in her bag.

"Aren't you invading their privacy?" I was not liking this one bit.

"The only way to get into the attic is through the living room, up the stairs to the second floor, and then up another flight to the attic. We're here. It's a long way to come to have to leave."

"What if they come home while we're in the attic?"

"I will explain that I emailed and left a message on their voicemail that we were coming, and that I was surprised they were not here."

I shrugged. "Let's go. Can't argue with your logic, and I do want to see this house."

"This isn't the original lock. You should have seen the key I had when I lived here. It looked like one a pirate would use to open the padlock of his treasure chest."

"I'm surprised you didn't save it, Mom."

"It might be in the stuff Dad stored for me when I . . . uh, went away."

We stepped into the entry hall, Mom quickly shutting down the alarm system.

"Wow! Look at that stairway." It was a gorgeous entry hall with its wood parquet floor polished to a high gloss. A brass and crystal chandelier hung from the vaulted ceiling making the space seem grand. The stairway curved up to the second floor, complete with a smooth hand rail and carved balusters.

"That oriental carpet is perfect for this place."

"That's mine, Annie. I have no place to put it in my apartment in the City. I like the tenants. I'm sure they'll take good care of it. Someday it will be yours and Ty's when you make a home."

"Mom, stop marrying me off," I said a little too sharply.

"Sorry," she said, biting her lip. "But you love Ty."

"We are not thinking about marriage. So please, stop. We have a lot of schooling to get through." This time my tone was gentler. I twisted Ty's ring around my finger several times.

On either side of the hall were rooms of equal size, one a living room, the other a dining room. Each had floor to ceiling windows facing out to the front lawn.

"Come and see the library and the kitchen," Mom beckoned.

The library had floor to ceiling bookshelves filled with books. Where there were no bookcases, the walls were adorned with paintings, mostly landscapes.

"The books come with the house and the paintings are your Gramma Carla's."

I noticed the wires around the window panes. "Now I see why the house is alarmed. Aren't you afraid the tenants will damage or walk off with this stuff?"

Mom smiled. "Tallie is a librarian. I had them thoroughly

investigated and I required a large security deposit. I have the most reliable house sitters because of the care I took checking them out."

Mom led the way down the hall, talking like a real estate agent. "The kitchen is totally uninteresting. It's a modern addition. When the house was built in 1812, most cooking was done in a separate building. The kitchen in the main house was a tiny affair with a large fireplace for providing heat and drying clothes in the winter."

We went up a different stairway behind the library, unlocking a door at the top. "There's a similar door at the top of the main stairway." We were on the second floor.

"Which one was your room?"

Mom pointed. "There's nothing in there. Let's go up to the attic." She obviously didn't want to visit her old room. We climbed a narrow set of stairs with another door at the top. It was hot and musty. The steps creaked under our weight, sounding loud and hollow in the silent house.

Mom opened the door to the attic. It was a large space, much bigger than I'd expected. It had a plank floor and two large dormer windows that looked out on the front lawn. The walls and peaked ceiling were unfinished. This space was filled with stacks of furniture, chairs, tables, bedsteads and old bureaus-all pretty cool looking antiques.

"Boy, I would love one of those bureaus for my apartment in Vermont."

"How about this one? This is the one I found the letters in." Mom opened the drawers. They were filled with photo albums and papers tied with string, or in folders.

"Look at all these photo albums." The drawer creaked with the heavy load of several old fashioned albums, each one wrapped in ancient yellowed layers of cellophane. The aroma of old perfume wafted to our noses. The scent tweaked a memory, but I couldn't nail down what it was.

"I don't know if we'll find anything of value here regarding what happened at Grumman in 1943," Mom said.

"Before we get lost in these albums, let's see what else is around," I said.

There were two trunks besides a dresser that had three more large drawers. I opened the top drawer and a large black spider cringed in the corner, right on top of the album I reached for. I blew gently on him, hoping he would move on.

"What is it, Annie?'

"Just a spider," I mumbled, trying to slip the album out without aggravating the critter.

"I took anything of value from the blue trunk. That's where I found the letters. Let's finish the trunks before we move on to the dresser," Mom said.

"How about that red one?" I pointed at an old fashioned steamer trunk. A large brown spider was spinning a long thread from a low rafter on the eave above us to the red trunk. Its spindly legs carefully climbing up the silk it had just released for the next spoke in the web.

"I'm going to try to open the trunk without disturbing Mrs. Spider and her web," I said.

"Really Annie? The spider has nothing better to do all day. We have to get out of here sometime today."

*So much for respecting nature,* I thought, carefully removing the strands of web from the trunk and sliding it away from the slanted ceiling.

"Back in 1943, this is what you would have packed your clothes in to go to college," Mom explained.

The trunk was locked. "Oh crap," I muttered.

"Don't lose heart. I have a set of keys here. I bet one of them fits."

She tried key after key. None worked. She settled back on her haunches and looked defeated.

"Uh, I might be able to help." I didn't really want to let her know I had these, but I fished in my bag for my set of lock picks.

"What are those? No. They're not what I think they are, my daughter. Where did you get those?"

"Um, Aunt J's friend, Lieutenant Red. It was a joke. He called me a junior sleuth after we discovered the art forgeries last year and gave them to me for my birthday."

"I see. Well, let's use them. It isn't exactly breaking and entering. I own all of this."

I went to work with the picks. Mom looked on with what I interpreted as dubious pride. After five minutes of trying, the old lock gave way. The trunk opened like a clam shell, scraping against the attic's dirty wood floor. An aroma of rusted metal from the screeching hinges, unused to being opened, drifted from the trunk. The now familiar smell of old fabric and yellowing paper permeated the air. I sneezed. Mom blew her nose.

"Is there a window we can open?"

"Over there," Mom pointed.

The window was painted shut. It reminded me of a horror movie I saw where a girl my age was lured into a house by an old woman who locked her in an upstairs bedroom with a window just like this one. I never could figure out why the girl couldn't break the window. *Okay, that's enough trying to find logic in old horror films. Back to work.*

"Look at all these newspaper clippings! Maybe we'll find something about Brenda McPhee in here." Mom was opening the drawers that were set into one side of the trunk.

"Do you think any of the women Great Gramma flew with are still alive? Maybe they know Charlotte or Brenda McPhee," I asked.

"I think we are going to find out at some point. Let's be careful with these. The paper is fragile, so old and yellow. Here. I found some cloth napkins in one of the dresser drawers." She began to lay them out carefully, a napkin between each article. Mom would make a good antiquarian.

"Mom, look at this photo." Four women in baggy trousers, leather jackets with fur collars and flight helmets walked toward the photographer. They wore jack boots and silk scarves and looked like they owned the world. The caption read, "*The*

*WASPS: Women take over the role of test pilots while their men fight the war."*

I was falling under their spell. It was a thrill getting to know about my great-grandmother, Charlotte, and her friends. I could only imagine what they must have felt, flying and testing the planes that won a war.

"Mom, we have to digitize this stuff."

"What is *digitize?*"

"You convert the documents and pictures to a computer file so you can save it all on the computer and actually enhance the photos. It's a skill I learned in my art course."

"I agree. These are historical records for our family. They must be saved."

The first clipping showed a group of five women sitting in a Jeep, parked under the wing of a plane I assumed was an Avenger. They looked, I don't know, proud, excited, confident and, yes, happy. They sported the leather helmets and flight jackets pilots wore back then. Each was carrying her parachute packs on her lap. Their goggles were pushed up on their helmets.

I tried to feel the significance of this photo, young women in the middle of a war, their guys off fighting somewhere. Why did they look so happy?

Mom broke into my thoughts. "These ladies must have been so proud to be able to help out in the war effort."

"Ah, that's it, Mom! That's why they look so happy. They were part of a great big picture."

The next series of articles showed women in factories, some in blue overalls and red bandanas I had seen in my history book that said, *"WE CAN DO IT!"*

One article listed the women's names and where they worked. Two were from the Grumman plant on Long Island.

"Mom, do you think we could try to trace these women?"

"Dunno," she said in a distracted voice. Mom picked up the next article. It was about the women who were test pilots for Hellcats and Avengers. Looking over her shoulder, I laughed. At the bottom of the page, one of the women was featured in an old ad for Camel cigarettes. "Who'd a thunk?!" I exclaimed.

"Smoking was considered glamorous," Mom said. "Watch some of the old movies. Some of the actresses were known for the way they held a cigarette and blew out the smoke. Women imitated them, trying to be as sexy as their female idols. Or is it idolettes?"

"I'm so glad you quit, Mom."

"Me, too. Let's see what else is here. We can pack the rest of these articles up, and read them at home. You look in . . ."

A door slammed somewhere on the second floor below us. Mom dropped what she was holding and froze.

"I'll go see who it is," I said.

Descending the steps from the attic to the second floor was no mean trick. They were steep, narrow and rickety. Landing in the hallway, I looked toward the door to the first floor. A woman in a flowered dress with blondish gray hair rolled into some sort of buns was just passing through that door. She slammed it behind her.

I shouted for her to wait. No answer. I ran to the door, opened it and followed the stairs to the first floor. It was completely silent. *Where had she gone?* I called out to say who we were. There was no answer.

Returning to the attic, lost in thought, I collided with my mother. "Oh God, don't scare me like that!" I blurted out. *Why was I so unnerved?*

"What did you see?" she said, ignoring my rapid raspy breathing.

"A woman. About your age. Dressed funny, flowery dress, odd shoes, strange hairdo."

"Did she say anything?"

"No. Is she your tenant? She looked too old and certainly not pregnant."

"This is going to sound crazy, Annie, but the same woman appeared last time I was here."

"What do you mean, literally *appeared*?"

"Well, she *dis*appeared, just like your lady. So, if she *dis*appeared, she must have *appeared*."

"Again, can't fight your logic. Let's get our stuff and go." I hummed the theme from *Twilight Zone* .

I sneezed again, several times, as we packed up the contents of the trunk and bureau. I bent to pick up the last bundle under the slanted part of the roof when the door slammed again, much louder than before. I jumped, hitting my head on the eave. A piece of paper fluttered in front of me as my vision cleared. The big brown spider almost landed on my nose as she spun away at a new web. I pocketed the little piece of paper, scooping it from where it had landed on my shoe.

I looked at Mom, whose eyes were wide as saucers, and said, "Let's get out of here."

We grabbed everything, locking the door with my pick rather than trying every key until we found the right one, and made our way down the rickety stairs as quickly as safety would allow. After peering around every corner, nervous as cats, we left the house. In the car, Mom hastily penned a note for Tallie, the tenant, telling of our visit.

"I'll put it in the mailbox," I offered.

Mom barely gave me time to slam the car door and buckle up before she peeled out of the driveway.

"Annie, what was on that little piece of paper?"

I pulled it carefully from my pocket. "It's a list." I read, "Flashlight, screwdriver, pliers, rubber gloves, camera, tape, charcoal powder, small paintbrush, ski mask, flask, cigarettes."

"Probably nothing," she murmured, signaling to turn onto the main road.

*Probably a kit to collect evidence*, I thought.

# CHAPTER 18

*Flying Home*

Ty had arrived at Carroll County Regional Airport too late to make it back to Long Island during daylight. He didn't want to make a night flight with so little experience relying solely on instruments.

Tom Ballard, the air strip manager, invited Ty to join him at a local diner for supper. He also generously offered Ty the cot in his office for the night. Ty accepted and texted Annie and Jazz Wiedermeier his plans.

Tom took Ty to a small homey restaurant in the town of New Windsor and proclaimed with a hearty back slap, "Buddy, you're in Maryland. You gotta try the crab cakes."

"Sounds good but it's my treat. Thanks for taking care of the plane and loaning me your cot."

"Deal!" said Tom.

"I have a strange story, Tom. You interested?"

"Shoot," Tom said as the waitress came to take their orders.

"I *am* hungry, and if the food is as good as it smells, I will be happy as a clam, or is it a crab?" Ty said, smiling up at the waitress.

The waitress smiled back, took their orders, and left.

"So what's this strange story?"

Ty missed having Annie to talk to about what they'd found at NCIS, and ideas came to him more easily when he could talk thing over with someone. Maybe Tom, who knew planes, would be a good person to bounce ideas off. So Ty began the story of Brenda McPhee and the plane crash in the Appalachians. He didn't mention Charlotte or the odd circumstances of her experiences at Grumman. Their food came and Ty put the story on hold until they finished eating.

"Wow. They don't make crab cakes like this in New York!"

Tom smiled around a mouth full of coleslaw. "You bet!"

"In my opinion," Tom said in response to Ty's detailing the findings about the crashed plane, "the easiest way to bring a plane down like that is to monkey with the fuel gauge."

"What do you mean? How?"

"If you know what you're doin', you can make the fuel gauge read a quarter full when it's empty. I set my fuel gauge to read empty when it's a quarter full. Just a way to remind me to fill 'er up. I'll show you when we get back to the field." Tom folded his napkin and changed the subject, "How do ya like that Cherokee Arrow? By the way, I did change the fuel for you. I didn't see anything that could have caused the hesitation in the engine, but just a little dirt or water can do that."

"I'm new at this, so I don't have anything to compare it to, but I'm having fun flying it."

"She's a good reliable bird, alright. What happened to your girl?"

"Annie had some business with her mom in New Windsor. They'll drive home tomorrow."

Ty paid the bill and dropped the rental car. Tom drove him to the airport and wished him a safe flight. Finally, after a night tossing and turning on the cot, Ty took off for Long Island.

As he flew home, Ty remembered what Tom had said about the fuel gauge. *Tom never showed me the fuel gauge trick. I will have to ask Jazz.* By the time Ty reached southern New Jersey, a light rain had started to fall. He radioed the tower at Republic Airport. The controller said the visibility was still good enough to land and, that there were no gusty winds.

Ty landed smoothly, his confidence growing with every flight. He taxied to the Cherokee's parking spot whereJazz met him as he jumped to the ground.

"Good flight? No more engine sputters?"

"Yeah, I love flying this plane. She behaved all the way home."

"She's a good 'un," Jazz admitted.

"I have a question for you, Jazz."

"Yeah, sure.What?"

"How do you tamper with the fuel gauge on a plane?"

Jazz looked at Ty, scratching his head, and then shook it. "What?"

"I know. It sounds crazy."

"It's not that easy unless you know what you're doing. I can show you some time. More importantly, my dad wants to talk to you and your girl about his time at Grumman. He's been funny ever since your visit. I think he's remembered some things that bother him.

# CHAPTER 19

## *Charlotte Takes Matters*

1943

*The finished planes were lined* up on the field waiting for pilots
to fly them to the Pacific bases. It was pitch dark, no moon at all.
The factory windows were blacked out too, even though shifts ran
twenty-four/seven. The greatest fear was that there would be an
air raid, and all the planes would be destroyed before they could
be used against the enemy.

Charlotte, dressed in dark clothes, a ski mask over her head,
waited in the shadows of a stairway used by the plane assem-
blers to climb onto the wings. Confirming her suspicions, a figure
emerged from the plant. From its appearance, Charlotte deduced
it was a man. He moved silently around the area where plane
parts were kept before being distributed to the assembly line inside.
He seemed to know what he was looking for, moving from one

*pile of parts to the next. Every so often he paused and dropped something into a canvas sack he carried.*

*What was he doing? And who was he?*

*The figure finally finished his work and went inside. Charlotte crept up to one of the stacks of parts. Only one box was opened. She checked the other stacks. Same thing. One box, same part.* Now I know why the bomb bay doors of some planes don't function properly! *Charlotte said out loud, then clamped her hand over her mouth, hoping no one had heard her.*

# CHAPTER 20

## *Letters, Letters, We've Got Letters*

Mom and I returned from New Windsor to find Ty sitting with Aunt J, having coffee in the kitchen.

"Aunt J, did Ty tell you about our flight to New Windsor?"

"Nope, Annie. I thought I would leave that to you." Ty said, planting a kiss, and hugging me.

"That was so much fun. When can we do it again?" I asked.

"Pretty special, just the two of us flying around in the clouds," he whispered as we left the kitchen and retrieved Charlotte's letters from the library. This next kiss was just for the two of us, alone and dreaming of our first flight. "We'd better get to work," he murmured in my hair.

Torn between staying in Ty's warm hug and finding the answers we hoped were in the letters, I said, "Yes, we are never going to solve this mystery unless we decode the rest of these letters." As we had decided before we left NCIS headquarters, the letters were definitely our best lead.

"We have the reports from NCIS, and all the other background stuff you found in the attic. It's all going to fit together," said Ty.

I had filled Ty in on the little note that fell from the eaves in Charlotte's attic and my feeling that it wasn't just a shopping list.

"If we could get the rest of the notes between Charlotte and Frank," Ty confirmed, "we might be able to prove your theory that the list you found was Charlotte's, and that she was trying to catch saboteurs."

"And don't forget the ghost," I said. Mom and I had analyzed everything that occurred during our visit to the attic in New Windsor. We couldn't explain the lady who liked to slam doors, so we decided to call her a ghost for now.

Mom interrupted. "I think we need to talk about what happened in the attic, Annie. It's the second time that woman, who we believe is Charlotte's ghost has slammed the door while I was there. This last time she actually led us to that little piece of paper. Ty and Jill, I would like to know what you think of this."

Jill looked down at the pile of letters. "I think she's leading you to clues. Every time you go to that attic you come back with something that proves to be important, or at least interesting."

Ty had leaned back against the chair Aunt J was sitting on, his long legs stretched out in front of him, eyes closed. "Were you afraid of her?" He opened his eyes to look from Mom to me.

"Yes," we said in unison.

"It was such a strong presence with all that door slamming," Mom said.

"It's as if she's angry at us," I added. "I'm not sure I'd ever go there alone."

"I want to meet that ghost. You know how good I am with ghosts." Ty smiled. He was referring to the ghost we had met on Fire Island the summer we met. His attempt at humor fell flat. The silence that followed gave no comfort.

Aunt J cleared her throat. "Okay. Here's the Latin text and the notes. We can lay them out in chronological order."

"Yes, the messages might make more sense to us that way," Ty agreed.

We used the same formula as before: the first number in the code referred to a page starting with the Latin word, *amo*, while the rest of the numbers were letter counts on the page.

Charlotte's first letter took us three minutes to decode. It said BOMB BAY DOORS.

We moved on to Frank's response. Our decoding formula didn't work on this one. It was gibberish. "Let's go back to the simple word count," Ty suggested. Again, no luck.

"How about simple page count, first word?" I said.

"Voila! That's it." It read BE CAREFUL.

"Do you think they changed the code every time they sent a letter?" Mom asked.

"We'll find out," Ty said. "Let's see if Charlotte used the same code every time."

Using her original code, Charlotte's next letter revealed EMPLOYEE TO BLAME. MALE.

Frank, true to form, used his code. SET A TRAP. TRUST WHO.

"How did she know that Frank would have the same Latin text book?" Ty asked.

"It's in the first letter. She asked him if he still remembered when she first told him she loved him. He wrote back that it's in their Latin text, in Latin, and that he'll never let it out of his sight. He said it connects him to home and to her."

"I guess I'm just too stuck on these numbers to pay attention to the people involved in this mystery. How in the world did she stop the saboteur?" Ty said concentrating on the next set of letters.

Charlotte said WE ARE SMOKING AND DRINKING ON THE FIELD.

Frank replied DON'T GET CAUGHT.

"I haven't a clue what this means," I said, yawning and stretching.

"Let's pick this up tomorrow. It's late," I said. We protected our project from Trouble and said our goodnight with a long hug, kneading each other's stiff muscles.

"Sleep well, Annie, and dream of me, huh, not the Cherokee," Ty whispered twisting my ring. I twisted it back.

I pulled him back to me and gave him another kiss, "Not to worry, Ty. I still like you better than the plane. Come back soon, okay?" I teased.

"Sure thing, Miss Tillery," he winked.

# CHAPTER 21

## *Charlotte Finds a Way*

1943

*"I found out why there* is a problem with the latch on the bomb bay doors. It's sabotage."

"How can you be sure?" Angie asked.

"I saw him switching the parts."

"Where?" Connie demanded.

"Well, haven't you been busy, lady!" Maxine added.

"I've been snooping," Charlotte admitted.

"Are you crazy?" chorused all three friends.

"No. I am very careful."

Charlotte and three of her best friends, Angie, Connie and Maxine had locked themselves in the ladies' room to discuss Charlotte's suspicions. There was a bang on the door. "It's out of order. Go upstairs," yelled Maxine.

"I need your help. I want to surprise this guy, so that he'll stop what he's doing."

"Who is he?"

"Dunno. For me, it's enough if he just stops. Truth is, I'm afraid to let him know we know there is something going on. He's a saboteur, so he must be dangerous. Here's the plan. Tomorrow night . . ."

---

The four young women met on the field. Each had made an excuse to leave their job, retrieved her bottle of "whiskey" from its hiding place, and slipped out through a rarely used door.

"He hasn't come out yet," Charlotte said. "Let's set up shop where he can see us. We need to let him hear us, too."

"But not enough noise to interest one of the security guards," said Connie.

They lit up their Camels and took swigs of the Coke they had put in the whiskey bottles. A few minute later, the same dark figure emerged from the factory. He went straight for the stacks of parts, which were renewed daily. The women giggled and flicked their Zippo lighters, an effort to make some noise and cause their cigarette ends to glow. Out of the side of her eye, Charlotte saw Mr. Saboteur shrink away into the shadows. She rose, announcing, "Let's go back in girls. Fun's over."

*The man disappeared into the building.*

*"C'mon. Inside. Before we're caught."*

*Sneaking back into the factory, the women looked for someone who looked or acted suspicious. Everything seemed normal.*

# CHAPTER 22

## *Journal Writing*

"Aunt J, I'm going to take a break from packing. Ty is coming over later, so we can finish decoding the letters."

I stood up, stretched to ease my back, and went into the library. The box of memorabilia Mom and I took from Charlotte's attic sat on the floor. Something moved inside the box and gave me a start. That near ghost experience in New Windsor had me a little jumpy. I crept up to the box, and yelped when Trouble shot out of the box with a piece of ribbon in her teeth. She fell to the floor, rolling over and meowing, so proud of her little souvenir.

"Hey, Trouble, what's up?" I scratched her chin and she started to climb up my jeans leg, a habit I think I need to put an end to. *What if she keeps this up when she weighs twelve pounds or more?* I thought.

On top of the pile of items in the box was one of Charlotte's journals. I picked it up and opened to the first page. It was dated *January, 1943* and was followed by a brief statement:

*Some of my observations about the war, my job and the people I loved and who loved me will live on in these pages. I dream that one day someone will find this, read it and make the pages live in their imaginings.*

"Well, Charlotte," I muttered, "You got your wish. And if I can help it, we are going to figure this out."

The first few pages described the procedures every WASP carried out before each flight. It reminded me of Ty's takeoff checklist.

The phone rang. "Darn it." I put Trouble down, trying not to drop the journal. No such luck. The journal started to slide to the floor, but I caught it. The jolt of stopping it mid-fall caused some small objects to fall from its pages.

Aunt J had answered the phone. I could hear her talking. She said, "Okay, Red. I'll be in tomorrow. We can follow that lead." After a pause she hung up. Red was Lieutenant Red Flaherty. He was like an uncle to me, the one who gave me the lock picks. He was also one of the best homicide detectives in my aunt's department.

Trouble was headed for the scraps that had fallen from the journal. I intercepted her just in time, sweeping her onto the chair. The little scraps were actually bits of cellophane tape, each about an inch wide and three inches long. I discovered that they had no sticky side. Someone had stuck two pieces of tape together. They looked dirty. I held one up to the light but couldn't make out the details. A brainstorm reminded me that there was a magnifying glass on the dictionary stand.

There were five pieces in all. I laid them out on a sheet of white paper near the desk lamp. The magnifying glass revealed that the smudges had patterns.

"Aunt J? Can you come here for a minute? I need your expert opinion."

"Ooh," I breathed. The penny dropped!

As Aunt J came up behind me, I demanded, "Look, look! What do you see?"

She peered at the little scraps for what seemed like an eternity before she turned to me with a strange look.

"Where did you get these, Annie? They're fingerprints."

# CHAPTER 23

## Detective Charlotte

1943

"What are you doing with that stuff?"

"I'm going to see if I can get some fingerprints." Charlotte had assembled a kit in a paper bag. It consisted of a small fat paint brush, some cellophane tape and fine charcoal powder she'd bought at an aquarium supply store.

"Do you want me to go with you?" Maxine and the rest of the women pilots were jumpy after Brenda's plane had disappeared.

"No, but stand guard at the door. If anyone shows up, just say real loud, 'Got an extra smoke. I'll come out to join you for one.' Then stall whoever it is so I can clean up my gear and light up."

"Will do."

Charlotte slipped out and found the stack of parts she had seen the shadowy figure messing with the previous night. She covered her head with a black cloth and, using a flashlight, set to work.

"Okay, spirit of Sherlock Holmes, show me some prints," she prayed. Carefully, just as it was described in the FBI manual, she lightly sprinkled the charcoal over the surface of the packing boxes. She waited a few minutes, and blew most of the powder away. There were lots of prints. She started to lift them by placing the cellophane tape over the prints the charcoal had revealed.

She was able to lift six prints when Maxine called out to her, "Hey, got an extra butt for me?"

"Sure, come on out."

Charlotte carefully stowed all her materials in her bag, popped a cigarette in her mouth and lit it. She'd just managed to stuff her kit and the black cloth under the rolling parts cart when Maxine showed up with Sarge Wiedermeier!

Charlotte suddenly realized that the telltale charcoal would be visible the next day to anyone who used the cart if she didn't clean it off. She leaned on the cart with her elbows, appearing to rest her back. Meanwhile she rubbed across the area she had dusted.

"Hi, Sarge." Charlotte smiled, as she tossed her pack of Camels to Maxine.

# CHAPTER 24

## *Dead End?*

I let Ty in, grabbing him by the arm and fairly dragging him into the den to see what I'd found in Charlotte's journal. "What do you think these are?" Aunt J had carefully taped the little pieces of cellophane onto a piece of plain white paper.

Squinting at them, Ty whistled, "Are they fingerprints? Where did you find them?"

"In a journal we brought from New Windsor." I explained how they fell out when I dropped the journal.

"Did the journal say whose they are?" Ty asked staring at the little pieces of tape.

"Not yet, but that list we found in the attic was Charlotte's crime scene kit. I knew it!"

"Let's get down to the rest of the letters. Maybe the answer will be in one of those messages." Ty took off his jacket and rolled up his sleeves. I flattened the next letter out on the table next to the Latin text and we put our heads together to finish the task, more excited than ever to find whose fingerprints Charlotte had discovered.

"Look at this one, Ty." I had decoded the next set.

Charlotte: MISSED MY FLIGHT. BRENDA'S PLANE DISAPPEARED.

Frank: CEASE AND DESIST.

Another soft whistle escaped Ty's lips. The triumph of decoding the messages was blunted by the deadly nature of their content. This was a sobering task.

"I wonder how that made Charlotte feel? Brenda was her friend. And, I bet she didn't *cease and desist*." Ty said.

"I would have wanted to find out what happened," I agreed. I flexed my fingers, not realizing how stiff they were from holding so tightly to the seat of my chair.

We worked on the next set.

Charlotte: SABOTEUR STOPPED.

Frank: SCARED OFF?

The next one proved to be a blockbuster.

Charlotte: I KNOW WHO IT IS.

Frank: PROOF?

Only one letter remained.

"There's a hospital bill here, Ty. It's for Charlotte, reporting her injuries. It says she suffered bruises, a black eye, and a broken arm as a result of being attacked at the Grumman plant."

"This just gets more dangerous for Charlotte with every piece we decode." I felt a sudden chill.

"Maybe there's something in the code about that. This is the last letter in the pack."

This letter was different. The stationery was formal and housed in a legal size envelope. I picked it up and removed the letter. "It's from the Navy. Oh, God, Ty. It's the letter informing Frank's parents that his plane went down while engaged in combat." I covered my face with my hands but couldn't stop the tears. Wiping my eyes with my sleeve, I looked up at Ty, who just stared at the letter, his glum face reflecting what I was feeling.

"I felt like I knew them. They were becoming friends almost," he said.

"Yeah." I blew my nose. "And I guess we'll never know who the saboteur was."

"Maybe the ghost knows, Annie. Do you think if we visited your Gramma's house we could scare her up for a pow-wow?"

"Scare her up? Really, Ty?" I made a face at his pun, but the wheels were already turning.

"By the way, Annie, Mr. Wiedermeier wants to see you. We've got a date to see him tomorrow."

"Really!" *Could he hold some piece of this puzzle?* I thought.

"He's got to know something, Annie. Just the way he shut us down on the last visit when we mentioned Brenda McPhee makes me believe he remembers more than he is letting on."

# CHAPTER 25

## The Unwitting Witness

1943

*Felix George Wiedermeier, better known* as Sarge, had very poor eyesight and a heart murmur. These conditions were enough to excuse him from the draft. His job at the Grumman plant on Long Island was labeled Security, but included other duties.

He was on the night shift this particular week. The supervisor had asked him to stay past his usual shift, which ended at 6AM, the time the lady pilots were dispatched.

No one was allowed out on the field when it was dark, except the crew that towed the finished planes to their designated spots on the field, awaiting their pilot. One good thing about the field was that you could smoke. Wiedermeier plucked a pack of Camels from his rolled up T-shirt sleeve and was about to flip open his Zippo lighter when he heard a scraping sound near one of the planes. It was barely audible. The hairs on his neck and arms stood up straighter than a Marine in a parade. His ears prickled as he attempted to detect a repeat of the noise.

Scraaaaaape!

This time he caught the direction of the sound. He padded softly toward a line of planes ready for tomorrow's flights. Another scrape and he was able to locate the plane. A dark figure stood near the tail end of its fuselage, his back to Wiedermeier.

He screwed up his courage. "Hey, Buddy. What's up there?"

The dark figure moved away from the plane and tossed a quick comment over his shoulder. "Just checking something for tomorrow. Everything is shipshape."

The voice was familiar, yet Wiedermeier could not place it. He went over and checked the plane for anything unusual. He noted the Avenger's ID. Nothing seemed unusual or out of place.

Still, that voice. If only he could place it.

# CHAPTER 26

## *Charlotte, Brenda and Mr. Wiedermeier*

"Let's review your latest finding from the attic, Annie. The ghost showed you the list of materials Charlotte took with her to catch the saboteur?" Ty asked.

"It's my theory. She slammed the door to make the note falling out of the eaves. That is, if it was Charlotte's ghost who slammed the door. I am hoping Mr. W . . ., uh, Felix, has something more solid to tell us."

"What do you think he's remembered? The rest of the coded messages in the letters gave us no clue about your little list," Ty noted.

"I guess we'll find out. Let's go," I urged.

We drove to the Wiedermeier home, moving at a maddeningly slow pace in the morning rush hour traffic. We had checked to make sure he was still up for chatting.

"I don't know. He seemed upset when you mentioned Brenda McPhee the last time we were here. I hope we don't give him a heart attack with the latest on Brenda."

"He looks tougher than that," I replied.

"What about his bad ticker?" Ty asked.

"Hmmm. Have a nitro patch on you, Dr. Ty?"

"Not a doctor yet, Sherlock."

We pulled up to the little cottage and Jazz met us at the door. Felix Wiedermeier was waiting in the kitchen. He looked stern, a determined expression narrowing his blue eyes and setting his mouth into a firm thin line.

"Hi, Felix. Glad to see you looking so well."

"Hi, yourself, Beautiful. And give me a handshake, Ty."

This friendly Mr. Wiedermeier was not what I expected after our last conversation. Mr. W and Jazz served tea and coffee cake. After a brief time spent munching, he cleared his throat. "I haven't ever shared this with anyone. First, I was afraid to tell anyone. I could've gotten hurt. I had a family to support."

Jumping in head first, I blurted, "Mr. Wiedermeier, do you know why Brenda McPhee's plane crashed?"

"Please, Annie, it's Felix. I only have suspicions. I don't know for sure. One thing I do know is your Charlotte was supposed to be in that plane, not Brenda. It was a mistake that Brenda was the pilot. Charlotte had gone back into the plant to check something. The dispatcher wanted to get the plane going and wouldn't wait for her to come back."

"Why do you think the plane was meant for Charlotte?"

"She was called first. Also Charlotte had been nosing around. She found something or was about to. No, I think she was meant to get into that plane and that it was meant to crash. My job at the plant was security, and sometimes I was the dispatcher sending the girls off to California. I saw a lot but the dispatcher that night was a new guy. I had never seen him before and I never saw him again. If he was supposed to get Charlotte on that plane, he blew it." Felix leaned forward. "You know she was mugged out in the field one night? What was she doing there?"

"Would you be willing to tell your story to the Navy? We have some letters from Charlotte and her boyfriend, Frank, that jive with your story." I didn't want to say too much, because all of the letters and stuff we were finding needed to go to NCIS.

"I didn't come clean in 1943 because I was scared. Now, I have nothing to lose," he answered.

*But what exactly had Charlotte found out? And, even more important, who were the bad guys?* I wondered.

Mr. W tipped his tea cup to his lips one more time, then placed it firmly and carefully in its saucer. Spreading his hands on the table, he looked from Ty, to me, then to Jazz.

"If I can be of any help, let me know. If NCIS or the FBI, or anybody wants to talk to me, I'm ready. I need to get this off my chest, sooner rather than later."

# CHAPTER 27

## *The Navy Weighs In*

We got back into Ty's Rav4 and drove in silence for a while. This was so much to process. We had so many clues but no idea who the saboteur was. The identity of the shadowy figure remained just there, in the shadows. I texted Aunt J to say we were on our way and that our interview with Felix was *very* interesting.

"Holy cow! How will we ever figure out who the mysterious dispatcher was? This is monumentally frustrating!" I grumbled.

"Yup." Ty drove onto the entrance ramp to the L.I.E. and we headed back to the City.

"Does it matter anymore?" I asked.

"Does what matter anymore?" Ty said.

"If we know, seventy years later, who the saboteur was."

"You heard what the doctor at NCIS said. They learn from every case, and I think, in fact- I know-justice never comes too late for folks like Brenda McPhee or Charlotte," Ty pointed out.

We arrived home just in time for dinner.

"I'm anxious to know what Aunt J will make of all this," I said as we rode the elevator, following the wonderful cooking odors all the way from the ground floor.

"Hey I got your text. You two have been busy. I want a progress report," she said.

"Gosh, that smells good, Aunt J. What are you cooking?" Ty followed the aromas into the kitchen. You could never fault Ty for his appreciation of good food.

"*Entrecote et pomme frits*," she said, laying something from a French restaurant menu on us.

"Steak! How does one cook a steak in an apartment kitchen, Detective Tillery? I am amazed." Ty grabbed a couple of platters from the kitchen and I tossed the salad.

"It's magic, Ty. I give away no secrets. Eat and enjoy," Aunt J proclaimed.

"Um, blue cheese dressing." I poured a liberal amount onto my salad.

"You are going to give these secrets to Annie before she leaves for Vermont. She'll have to cook at times, you know," Ty said winking at J.

"Uh, I wasn't planning on cooking, Ty. I have a meal plan on campus."

"Oh." Ty's look of disappointment sent Aunt J and me into gales of laughter.

"You know, you can always do the cooking yourself, Ty."

The sound of human voices had brought Trouble out. She climbed up Ty's jeans-clad leg and peered from his lap at the table full of food.

"Aunt J, look how cute she is." I did my best to keep from giggling.

"She is NOT getting up on this table, Annie."

"Okay. She's just on Ty's lap."

Ty picked Trouble up gently and placed her in the big front pocket of his sweatshirt. She stuck her head out, purring and blinking up at Ty.

Dinner eaten, dishes done and coffee served in our library den, Aunt J demanded to know what we had uncovered since the day my Mom arrived with the letter from the Navy.

"We cracked the code in the letters, so you know that part. Ty's a genius with codes."

"Still, let's sum it all up," Aunt J suggested.

"Okay, Charlotte Wheeler suspected that sabotage was happening at the Grumman plant. She was able to figure out that faulty hinges for the Avenger's bomb bay doors were being randomly replaced for the good hinges, by someone who had access to the plant. Charlotte and her buddies checked all the planes and prevented the faulty parts from being switched. They did their best to stop the saboteur, things got rough and Charlotte was attacked one night while she was waiting to catch him in the act."

Aunt J looked puzzled. "How come he could replace the

parts? I thought these defense plants worked twenty-four/ seven during the War. The place would have been crawling with workers, and what about security?"

"It seems the parts for the planes were out in the field where the finished planes were parked which was very dark because of the stiff blackout regulations." Ty explained, picking up the story. "Remember, the Axis knew where our plants were, and the fear of an air raid was real."

"And I think from what Mr. Wiedermeier told us, some security people had to be involved," I added. "He told us Charlotte was attacked out in the field. That's what makes us think that the sabotage was happening out there, in the darkness of night, not in the plant which, as you said, was like a humming bee hive."

"Who, exactly, is Mr. Wiedermeier?" Aunt J asked.

"He worked at the Grumman plant at the same time as Charlotte. Just a lucky break to find him. He's the father of the guy Ty rents his plane from."

"You said it. Lucky break!" Aunt J agreed. "And your trip to Washington?"

I cleared my throat. "They verified the identity of the pilot, Brenda McPhee. She was one of Charlotte's friends. Mr. W thinks Charlotte was supposed to be in that plane but had gone back into the plant for something and missed her place in line. We are waiting for one more report from NCIS forensics, the chemical analysis of the fuel in the plane, as well as the analysis of what the instruments read at the time of impact. So far, they have not found any mechanical system to blame for the crash."

As I paused to take a sip of Aunt J's excellent Cappuccino, Ty continued the story. "The investigation is not complete. Wiedermeier thinks it was sabotage for sure, because Charlotte and her buddies were effectively preventing the use of the faulty bomb bay door hinges. Why else would Charlotte have been attacked? We need to verify that part of the story, though."

"What did you and Carol find in New Windsor, Annie?"

"A ghost." *Why mince words?*

"Oh, here we go again! Anything in the realm of the concrete?"

"Lots of great old photos, lots of newspaper clippings. We still have to go through all of it. But I think the most important thing we found was the names of Charlotte's sister pilots. She kept a journal. We can see if any of them survived. They may know something that gives us a clue about the saboteurs."

"So, you have leads. That's so important with a cold case. Let's hope the leads aren't just dead ends, literally and figuratively."

"What happens, Aunt J, if none of the leads pan out?"

"It will either be declared a closed case because of what has been found so far, or they will decide to pursue it until we know who the saboteurs were."

"What are the chances of finding that out after all these years?" Ty asked.

"All depends on the leads, Ty. Now, tell me about the ghost."

"I'll tell you what I saw." *What was it Mom and I saw? I* wondered.

# CHAPTER 28

## *Give It Just a Ghost of a Chance*

The doorbell rang.

"Mom! Just in time!" I said, pulling open the door, and giving her a kiss. "We're in the library trying to make sense of what we have so far. Coffee?"

"Maybe tea?" Mom put the huge tote she always seemed to be carrying on the floor in the library.

Jill served up the tea with some cookies. Mom sat, the tea cup balanced on her knee and patted her tote. She seemed to shine with the anticipation of what she had brought with her. I liked this change in her.

"You look like the cat that swallowed the canary," Aunt J said.

"Well, I think I found some important leads. I've been looking through Charlotte's journal."

I broke in, "You and me both. But before we get to that,

Mom, who was that woman we saw at the house in New Windsor?"

She looked down at the tote and rubbed her finger across its smooth red leather, as if trying to conjure an explanation. "I think it was my great-grandmother, Charlotte Wheeler."

I stared at her. "Mom," I said in the chiding voice one reserves for kids who are making things up.

"I know. I know. Sounds weird. Thing is, I recognized her. Remember, I knew her."

"But you were so young when she died."

"I remember the flowered dress. She wore it at my birthday party. I was very young, but I remember that dress," Mom insisted.

"Could someone be playing a trick?"

"Why would anyone be playing a trick on me? I doubt there is anyone left in New Windsor from way back then."

"Are you sure?"

"Oh, Annie. I'm not senile. I didn't drink my brain into dementia either. Don't you think I've given this some serious thought?" Her lip trembled and she looked toward the window. She turned to me, reached out for my hand and said, "I'm sorry I snapped at you, but I get tired of dealing with everyone walking on eggshells about my sanity."

"Yes, I'm sorry, too. It hasn't been easy. The fact that we both saw the lady in the flowered dress proves your brain hasn't turned to mush."

Aunt J refilled our cups and the uncomfortable moment passed.

"If it is Charlotte, why is she appearing to you now? What is she trying to tell you, or us?"

"I followed her the first time I saw her. She just wasn't anywhere in the house. I looked everywhere."

"Maybe she just needed to slam the door and make that piece of paper fall from the eaves the last time you were there," Ty suggested.

"That's an idea. Maybe it's more important than we think." Mom admitted.

"Do you think the tenant has ever seen the ghost?" I asked.

"Now that you ask, I received a very confusing note from Tallie, my tenant. She said she saw me walking down the hall from the attic and didn't know why I didn't stop in to say hello. Now that I think of it, it was probably her polite way of asking why I didn't say I was there in the first place."

"It wasn't you, was it?"

"I hadn't been there at all. I was in New York on the day she said she saw me. I didn't own up to being there, so Tallie thinks I'm senile, too. When you saw Charlotte's photograph, Annie, you said how much I look like her. I have no explanation for what Tallie saw, or what we saw. Do you? Annie? Ty? Jill?"

"Do you believe in ghosts, Carol?" Jill asked.

"I don't know. Why not? There are stranger things."

"Do you think we should go back to New Windsor to see if she appears again?" I said.

"You know, Annie, we have lots of leads here to track down." Mom patted the tote again. I would save Charlotte's ghost as a last resort."

A chill passed over me. *Charlotte is trying to tell us something,* I thought. I had acquired a deep and abiding respect for ghosts from my first encounter with the Fire Island ghost. I looked at Ty and our eyes met. He seemed to be reading my thoughts.

The moment passed and Ty offered, "That sounds like a plan. Let's see what's in that tote, Ms. Wheeler."

"Oh, just Carol, Ty. Ms. Wheeler? It sounds so formal." She smiled at him.

Carol placed the information she had brought in the tote on the library table. "This is going to take a lot of work. Annie, can Dad help? Randall has access to all kinds of files, and all these people I pulled from Charlotte's journal must have had top secret clearance."

It was true. Dad's job at the State Department gave him the ability to find information on just about anyone who had ever worked for the government, like the WASPS.

Mom continued, "By the way, have you heard anything further from NCIS?"

"Let me check." I refreshed my email and scrolled down through my new messages. There it was.

"Print it," Ty said.

I handed the copy to Mom, and we gathered behind her to read the message. My eye was instantly drawn to a sentence that read, *Our analysis of the fuel tank residue revealed the presence of sucrose, commonly known as table sugar. This would have caused catastrophic engine failure.*

This was followed by a series of three terse sentences: *There is no evidence indicating faulty information from the instruments. The investigation points to the cause of the plane crash as adulteration of the fuel. The presence of sugar in the fuel had to be introduced maliciously, as sugar is not found as a normal contaminant in airplane fuel.*

# CHAPTER 29

## *Charlotte and Company*

"Well, if we weren't motivated before, this email did the trick!" Aunt J declared. There was nothing like an official report from a forensics team to get her on board.

All the evidence was pointing to sabotage, but how were we going to find the bad guys after all this time?

Mom emptied the tote. Several notebooks tumbled out, much like the ones we used in elementary school. The white parts of the black and white composition book were yellowed with age and someone had filled in parts of the white designs with red ink.

"Are the notebooks dated?" Ty asked.

"Yes."

"Should we each take a few?" Aunt J offered.

Mom distributed the notebooks and Jill grabbed paper and pens, clearing away the coffee paraphernalia. The room grew quiet. Aunt J turned on more lamps. We hadn't noticed that evening had arrived. The room filled with the smell of old paper again as each of us opened a door to the past. Scrawled in these familiar looking composition books were the stories of the most exciting women of their time.

"Can't say Charlotte was much of a writer," I said, swatting at Trouble, who thought the notebooks might offer some interesting cat stories. "Are the entries in yours written in strings of single words?"

"Yes. There's not much here that I can figure out. Let's just concentrate on the few weeks around Brenda's crash."

"What's that date again?"

"June 12, 1943." Mom produced the notebook covering that time period and opened it.

"All the pages for the month of June are torn out!" she gasped.

"That can't be a coincidence, or some random act," Jill noted.

"This is a dead end for now. Let's look through the other stuff, and see if she kept an address book with names," I said.

"We can easily find the names of Charlotte's co-workers," Jill said. "They'll be in the Grumman files and the newspaper articles."

"Tracking these ladies down may not be so easy," she added. "They are either very old or deceased by now."

After an hour of poring through the notebooks, auto-graphed photos and newspaper articles, we had a list of names consisting of three pilots: Maxine Flynn, Angeline Becker and Connie Faber and, a shift foreman, Edie Frank.

"Let's fax this information to Dad."

Mom nodded but asked, skeptically, "What do you think any of them can tell us? What will they remember? Don't you think they would have told somebody what they knew years ago when it would have helped?"

"If we find any of them alive and willing to tell their story, we'll know. Otherwise, it's a dead end," Jill said.

We closed our notebooks, lost in our own thoughts about these women and what they might know.

# CHAPTER 30

## *Anatomy of a Saboteur: The Shadowy Figure*

Dad was delayed from returning to his post in Istanbul, providing him with the time to come to our apartment to see the evidence we'd collected first hand. He was as intrigued as we were, having completed the searches we had requested about Charlotte's saboteur. He opened the envelope with the no longer classified Grumman records he'd been able to access for us. He listened to the questions we asked. "What about sabotage in defense plants in WWII? What are we looking for, a Grumman employee, or some outsider? How would an outsider gain access to the Grumman plant? Who were Charlotte's buddies?"

Dad paced for a time, placing the Grumman material on the library table where he thought it would fit in with our decoded notes, Charlotte's list, the fingerprints she'd collected and her journals. After a time, as we looked on, he offered his theory. "The saboteur was never on the Grumman role of employees. He just disappeared after he realized Charlotte and Company were on to him. His plan to kill Charlotte failed when she missed the plane. After an investigation into Brenda McPhee's missing plane got under way, things just got too hot."

Dad's theory of how the saboteur had gotten into the plant was based on a report he read about one of the male factory workers who was found dead in his apartment. The cause of death was deemed natural causes, but strangely coincided with the presence of the shadowy figure at the plant. Dad surmised that the shadowy figure killed the worker, stole his ID and used it to gain access to the plant. Because he only needed it for a short period of time, there was nothing in the report about the dead employee missing an ID. His body was found well after the saboteur disappeared, because no one had reported him missing, since his ID showed up on the employee roles every day.

The dates are what tipped Dad off to this possibility. The facts we had uncovered included the estimated time of death of the employee, the dates in Charlotte's notes and letters to Frank that indicated suspicion of sabotage. Factor in the date of Brenda's disappearance and the date Mr. Wiedermeier claims he no longer saw the shadowy figure, aka saboteur, and it all seemed to coalesce into a perfect storm in favor of his theory.

"Wow, Dad. Those Grumman records were just what we needed to put all our pieces together," I said.

"We still have no idea who this saboteur is though," Aunt J pointed out. "We started out with the narrow field of possible Grummanites and now we have the entire worldwide field of all of spydom."

"That's where you should start," Dad suggested. "There will be a lot of unclassified material and newspaper articles for you to check for spy activity on Long Island. You have a very narrow time frame and that should help you. Let me know if you need more help when you find something more specific. But I have a plane to catch in the morning, and some work to file with the State Department. I loved seeing you all."

Dad shook hands with Ty and gave him a man hug. He kissed Mom, Aunt J and me, giving us all hugs too. I saw him to the door. "Don't worry, Annie. I have perfect faith you four will crack this mystery."

"I love you, Dad." He was out the door and gone. I went back to the library where the note reading and paper shuffling was in full progress. The new spin Dad put on the case had energized us.

# CHAPTER 31

## *Frank + Charlotte = Carla*

### The Missing Pages

The evening was young. Aunt J offered to make more tea and coffee, and we decided to press on with our investigation into Charlotte's life. Ty stoked the fire to life on the hearth. I sharpened pencils and we got to work.

This was puzzling me. "Mom, if Carla, my grandmother, your mother, was Charlotte's daughter, who was Carla's father?"

I could have asked if the Pope had a wife, and there would have been a less uncomfortable silence.

Mom cleared her throat and began, "Before Frank left for the war in the Pacific, he and Charlotte went to Bermuda for what they hoped would not be their last time together, war being what it was. The result was Carla, my mother. Charlotte told Carla that she and Frank were married in Bermuda, but there was never a marriage certificate to be found. Perhaps they were married."

"How do you know this?" I asked.

"Charlotte was very proud of Frank, especially after he was killed in the war. She wanted Carla to know what a great guy he was. She told her countless stories about Frank, their relationship, and manufactured a story about their romantic wedding in Bermuda. We all knew the story, but didn't know if it was true. After Charlotte was killed in the plane crash, my mother went through all the papers you and I rescued from the attic and didn't find a marriage certificate."

"That doesn't mean they weren't married. Maybe there's a record in Bermuda."

"I don't think it matters anymore," Mom said. "My mother kept his memory alive by telling me all about him, giving me his pictures and his war memorabilia."

I felt like a big door had opened in my mind, and I was being led into a room full of light and color. This was my family history, the one I never knew about.

"So, you get your sense of adventure and reckless disregard for danger from your great-gramma and her husband." Mom smiled and tucked a lock of my hair behind my ear. I looked down at Trouble to hide my welling tears.

Wiping my face on my sleeve, I said, "Mom, this is fantastic!" I reached over and hugged her. "What a gift! Most people know their grandparents. I never did."

"I have more," Mom said, reaching into the other large

shopping bag she had brought. It was a baby book Charlotte had kept about Carla, from birth to age seven. I opened it and a small key fell out.

"Does this fit anything you know about, Mom?'

She frowned. "No, but there are more boxes back in the attic, and diaries, too. I just couldn't carry it all. There's a jewelry box as well."

"They could hold the information we need," Jill spoke up.

"We need to get them. We can fly down and pick them up," Ty offered.

"There could be more pieces to this puzzle. I can't help but feel that Charlotte knew who put the sugar in the fuel tank, and why."

Mom frowned at this. "Why didn't she blow the whistle?"

# CHAPTER 32

## *Last Chance for a Ghost*

Time was running out. Ty and I were due in Vermont in a week, but this visit to the attic could provide us the clue we needed.

"How are we going to find Charlotte's friends, meet with them, search the attic AND finish packing in time?" I mumbled as we pulled up next to Jazz's hangar. He stepped out to meet us and, with his help, Ty checked out the plane as I observed. Knowing about Charlotte and her brave friends made me want to know what I needed to do to be a safe passenger as Ty piloted the plane. Mom went into the hangar to use the restroom.

"Hey, Jazz. Did Mr. Wiedermeier remember anything else?"

"I'll ask him, Annie. I tell ya though, he feels a lot better for gettin' that whole story about the lady pilots off his chest."

"Whatever he remembers could be vital to finding the saboteur," I said.

The plane checked out. Mom and I got in as Ty filed a flight plan with Jazz.

"You okay in that back seat, Mom?"

"Sure. I love flying in these little planes. Must be in the blood." She tackled the seat belt and arranged her headset.

"You're good to go, Ty. I'll pull out the wheel chocks. You have the tower man on the radio?"

Ty gave a thumbs up and we taxied away from our parking spot toward the runway. I could hear the tower giving Ty instructions for take-off, and he lined up at the end of the runway.

The early fall sky was clear blue with cumulus clouds casting shadows on the terrain below as we ascended. Ty flew the plane, checking instruments and I crossed my fingers, hoping the little plane would not give us another scare.

Mom watched the scenery below for a while then seemed to be making a list of some sort. She spoke, "I'm outlining what we've found so far. When I finish, take a look and see if you can add anything."

Her list was thorough: the coded messages from the love letters, the letter from NCIS, Brenda McPhee's autopsy report from NCIS, the analysis of fuel and instruments from NCIS, Mr. W's story, the little key from the baby book and the list of Charlotte's sister pilots from Grumman.

The detective living inside my head mulled over what we knew so far. *Sabotage was attempted at the Grumman plant in 1943. Charlotte and her friends were on to it, causing the saboteur to attempt to eliminate Charlotte, because she and her buddies were thwarting his plot. The sabotage stopped, but no saboteur was apprehended.*

Then I considered what we didn't know. *Who is the saboteur? Why didn't Charlotte and Company blow the whistle, or did they?*

We landed at Carroll County Regional Airport again and got a ride to New Windsor from one of Tom Ballard's friends.

This time Tallie was home and let us in.

"I'm leaving for work, Ms. Wheeler. Just lock up when you go. Thanks."

"Wait till you see the attic, Ty," I said, giving a witch's cackle.

He rolled his eyes. "This is a spooky house, I must admit," Ty observed, testing each of the rickety steps as we climbed to the attic door.

Everything was as we left it. The dust was disturbed where we had moved trunks and dressers. There were several sets of footprints left, no doubt, by us. I peered at the prints, trying to see how many different shoes were involved.

Reading my mind, Mom said, "Forget it, Annie. Ghosts leave no footprints."

"Right," I giggled.

"Okay, let's think this through," Ty said. "Ms. Whe . . ., ah, Carol, do you have keys to all these boxes?"

As Mom dug into her purse, Ty posed a plan. "What if the key fits something inside one of these boxes, like a diary? The key is small enough."

I lined up the boxes, sneezing several times. We tried each of Mom's keys. As we eliminated each box and its contents, we put it aside.

Finally we got lucky! A sturdy wooden box opened with one of Mom's keys. Inside was a much smaller box, beautifully inlaid with tiny sea shells. The little key fit nicely. Inside we found what Charlotte had kept secret all these years.

Suddenly one door slammed, and then another.

"There it goes again, Mom!" I ran to the hallway just as the last of that flowered dress disappeared. "Wait!" I yelled, as if a ghost would do my bidding. "Who are you?"

Another door slammed.

"That's the door to my old room," Mom said, wide-eyed. "Let's go!"

We rushed towards the room and stepped in the doorway. Our ghost was gone, but a picture in Mom's old bedroom had fallen to the floor from the force of the slamming door. Taped to the back of a print of this very house was a newspaper clipping. Careful not to shred the delicate old newsprint, Mom lifted it off the back of the picture frame. We huddled together to read it.

*June 12th, 1942, <u>U-Boat Sighted Off Long Island's South Shore</u>*

"What does this have to do with anything?" I asked.

"Let's see what's in the little box." Mom said, urging us back to the attic. "If this ghost is Charlotte, she is doing her best to get her story out."

We raced back to the attic. Inside the little box sat the curious collection of items listed in the note that fell from the eave on my first visit. There was a tiny paintbrush, tape, charcoal powder and a cellophane envelope containing index cards with what were obviously sets of fingerprints.

"This is where the scraps of tape Aunt J said are fingerprints came from!" I shouted, excited to see it all coming together.

On the back of each index card there was a date and another unknown marking, maybe a location. This was valuable. With her amateur little kit, Charlotte had gotten some fingerprints. My guess was that they belonged to the saboteur. *Where did you get them from, and were the ones we found in your journal from the same source?* I thought, imagining Charlotte.

# CHAPTER 33

## *Charlotte Gets Mugged*

1943

*Charlotte pulled a black turtleneck* sweater over her head. It covered what her blue overalls and black work shoes did not. Black gloves and scarf covered all but her face.

"Here. Tie this on bandit-style," Maxine ordered.

"Can you tie it, please? My hands are shaking too much."

"If you're that scared, how are you going to do it?"

"Because I'm the brave one. Courage is when you do what you have to, even if you're scared."

"No lectures, please. Just get in and get out, and get it done."

"Is the coast clear?" Charlotte wished she didn't have to do this.

"Go!" hissed Maxine.

Charlotte slipped out of the large closet they had been hiding in and through the exit door, leaving the busy plant behind. Outside in the field, Charlotte was enveloped in a fog. She leaned against the wall and closed her eyes. Thirty seconds later, eyes adjusted, she approached one of the carts with the plane parts. For just a second her tiny flashlight winked on.

There. A box with a tampered seal.

She stuffed the box into one of her canvas bags and, with fumbling fingers, went through the pile. Two more unsealed boxes. Two more went into the sack. Three sealed boxes came out of her other sack.

Too much noise! Charlotte quieted herself and listened. She went to the next cart and repeated the task. Ten carts in all. At the ninth cart, something caused a momentary, almost imperceptible brightness that paralyzed her. She dropped one of the boxes. As she bent down to retrieve it, a pain like none she'd ever felt traveled from her neck to her limbs. She heard a shoe scrape behind her. She opened her mouth to yell. Maxine was just on the other side of the door. Another blow across her back turned the yell into a yelp. Another blow across the back of her legs and she could only cover her head, waiting for the next one. If only she could turn to see who it was, but her vision erupted in blue dots and stars with each blow.

And then someone was yelling at her. "Charlotte! Oh, God! Charlotte!" Maxine and Angeline were patting her face. She looked up, putting her arms up defensively.

"Thank God, she's not dead," Angeline hissed. "Let's carry her in."

"No, we can't let anyone know what she's been doing," Angeline pointed out.

Charlotte mumbled, "She's right. We're not supposed to be out here, but we don't know if my attacker is inside. We can't let anyone see me like this. Help me up."

"Do you think you have any broken bones?"

Charlotte pushed them away and got up, swaying and groaning. "Take me to my aunt's house. She's a nurse. She'll help us and keep it quiet."

"We should report this!"

"To whom? Until we know who to trust, we need to keep quiet and catch this guy next time."

"Maybe he'll stop, now that he knows we're on to him," Maxine said.

"Let's hope so," Charlotte groaned, stopping to throw up.

"He could've killed you!"

"Yeah. Me, instead of the pilots whose planes got the faulty hinges."

# CHAPTER 34

## *Randall and Doc Have an Idea*

The flight home was uneventful and I wasted no time getting in touch with Dad. I hit his number on speed dial on our way home.

"Hi, Dad. I have a question."

"And how are you today, Annie?"

"Oops, sorry. I'm just, well, Dad, we've come up with something else, but we don't know where to go with what we've found."

"Those names you sent me? I'm still working on them, Annie. They may be the lead you need."

"You're a poet, Dad."

"What?"

"Lead you need?"

"Annie, maybe you need a short rest."

"Dad, we've found out a lot about Charlotte and her friends. Charlotte was collecting evidence about a saboteur, but there is nothing to indicate who it was, or if they were arrested. Could it be the saboteur was arrested, but that it was kept secret to protect an investigation into a larger espionage ring?"

"That's a very good theory, my girl."

"But how can I find out? Are there arrest records in the Grumman personnel files? Can they be accessed by us?"

"I'm not sure, Annie."

"Hey, what about Doc Egan?" I asked.

"He would know how to access that information, if it even exists, and if it's been declassified," Dad said. "I think Doc Egan's your man. Meanwhile, I'll get the contact information for those four women from Charlotte's journal."

"Even better, Dad. We found two sets of fingerprints. One was in one of Charlotte's journals and the other in a locked box in the attic. Why would she have those fingerprints? We think they may belong to her saboteur."

"I can help you with that one, too. Fed Ex them right away. You might break this case yet, Annie."

I said goodbye and checked my backpack for the little box with the precious prints inside. They were safe and as soon as I called Ty, I planned to Fed Ex them.

I had Ty on speed dial. He answered on the first ring. "Ty, hi. Can you get in touch with Doc?"

"Hello to you, my Annie."

"Sorry. My manners have deserted me. I just spoke with my dad about our new clues. He said that Doc might know how to access records that can tell us who our shadowy figure, aka, Mr. Saboteur, is."

"Why didn't I think of that?" Ty responded.

"That's my line," I replied.

"Doc just happens to be at Windalee on Fire Island. I was going to suggest we pay him a visit before we leave for Vermont." "Cool! I would love to see Doc, and Windalee. When?"

"Tomorrow. Early. I'll pick you up at 6AM. I love you."

"And I am crazy nuts about you, Ty." I rushed out to Fed Ex the prints. I was in such a hurry I forgot to tell Ty what Dad had said about the prints.

# CHAPTER 35

## *Return to Windalee*

"How special is this, Ty. I'm starting a new life with you in Vermont, AND we get to visit where we fell in love."

"Yeah, I love this place, Annie."

We stood locked together on the top deck of the ferry, watching the details of Fire Island emerge. Doc met us on the ferry dock and we walked the short distance to his cottage, called Windalee.

The autumn chill had set in on the barrier island. Doc, Ty's uncle, had a nice fire in the hearth and a steaming pot of coffee ready for us.

"What's up, kids? Ty told me about your great-grand-mother and her saboteur. How's your investigation going?"

"We think you can help us, Doc." Ty made it simple. He and his uncle communicated with simple uncomplicated words, reducing everything to its essentials.

"We need to find out who worked at Grumman when

Charlotte discovered the sabotage. How could we access those records?"

Doc began the ritual of filling and lighting his pipe, his brow knitting with the intricacies of the task. This was a sure sign that he was giving our problem his best mental gymnastics. When he was satisfied with the smoke curling above his head, he looked up. We both knew better than to disturb the process and sat like two obedient Golden Retrievers until he was done.

"We can contact Grumman," he said, "but I'm kind of a WWII spy aficionado, as it were. I've also worked many times with Alice D'Elia. You remember Alice. We've been collecting material for years on Long Island's WWII history. The aviation industry played a very important role, but we've been concentrating on other aspects, especially the German U-boat activities off our shores during the war. Sightings were made from Brooklyn's Sheepshead Bay to Amagansett on the East End."

Doc never failed to impress. Next to Aunt Jill, he was definitely my hero when it came to the art of investigation.

"Let me call Alice. She has most of what we've collected."

It was so nice to see Doc, my Santa Claus on Weight Watchers, complete with snowy hair and beard. AND those red suspenders. He brought Ty up after Ty's mother died and his father was put into rehab for alcoholism. After Doc retired from the CIA, he moved to Fire Island and restored the lovely New England style beach cottage we were visiting. Fire

Island was nothing more than a big sand bar. The Atlantic Ocean roared on one side and the gentle Great South Bay lapped against its shores on the other. Autumn turned the island crimson from the Virginia creepers and poison ivy. Deer roamed freely through the thickets of pine, holy and beach grasses. When you could cut out the sound of the surf by crouching in the dunes, the only sound was the constant breeze softly whistling in your ears.

Windalee sure had some mysteries of its own. This is the special place where Ty and I shared our first mystery. We lost Aunt Jill, we found a ghost, and some of Doc's neighbors tried to kill us. It was the most cool summer vacation I ever had.

Alice D'Elia was born on Fire Island and was one of its most respected historian and ghost hunters to boot. Both she and Doc were small children during WWII, and devoted themselves to unraveling some of the mysteries of their childhood.

"The whole country was at war and I want to know about my family's part, here on Fire Island," Alice had shared.

The storm door banged shut and Alice made her entrance. She liked to say she had a dramatic soul, and that she had probably been an actress on the British stage, a Russian princess, or a suffragette in some of her former lives. I guess that covers all bases.

"Annie! Ty!" She bestowed kisses and hugs upon us and a pat on the shoulder for Doc. She arranged her flowing purple cape around a straight-backed kitchen chair. Alice was tall with gray braids wrapped intricately around her head. Her outfit included a long flowing dress in a vivid shade of purple and a lot of gold chains and bangles.

She turned to us and said, "Wuzzup?" She cracked me up, switching from professorially perfect King's English to talking like some rock celebrity.

"You were definitely an actress in some former life." Ty said, winking at me.

Doc coughed and puffed on his pipe.

"Doc. Where are Merlin, super dog, and those wonders of the feline world, Punch and Judy?" I asked.

"Back in Boston. I'll be closing up soon, so I left them with a sitter."

Alice broke in. "Okay, what's this about? What crime are we trying to solve here? Doc gave me the barest of details. Your great-gramma, named Charlotte Wheeler, was trying to catch a saboteur at a defense plant where she was working as a WASP. Is that right so far?"

"That's it in a nutshell, Alice, but there's more to it. The real mystery is the identity of the saboteur and where he or they disappeared to. They were responsible for killing one of the lady pilots. It should have been Charlotte but, lucky for her, another woman, Brenda McPhee, flew in her place. Charlotte collected some fingerprints, which we found in the attic. We think they may belong to the saboteur. I sent them to Dad."

"How did you find out about Charlotte's counter-espionage activities?"

"Mom got a letter from NCIS about a note left in a plane that crashed in the Appalachians on its way to California in 1943. The note was traced to Charlotte, and then to my mother. Mom decided to go back to the family home in Maryland to see what she could find. The attic proved a treasure trove, especially the letters Charlotte exchanged with her fiancé, Frank Bradenton. The letters contained a code and Ty decoded them, with my help, of course."

"Annie and her mom provided the key to the code in the form of an old Latin textbook they'd found in the attic," Ty added.

"Phew!" Alice said. "That's quite a story. I need all the details in order to see how I can be of help. You know, there was a lot of espionage activity here on Long Island."

"And Alice, you may be interested to know: there is a GHOST." Doc winked at us through his cloud of smoke.

# CHAPTER 36

## *Spies, Plots and Terror*

For the next hour and a half Ty and I mapped out what we knew in the form of a timeline. We showed Alice and Doc how we decoded the letters, shared Mr. Wiedermeier's testimony about what he observed in 1943, and recounted NCIS's findings about the crashed Avenger and Brenda McPhee, its pilot. We also told them about the fingerprints found in the New Windsor attic that we had sent to my dad for identification. Finally, we told Alice about the ghost.

"You two have done good work!" Doc said. "You could easily get a job at the CIA."

Alice appeared lost in thought. At last she said, "Clearly, whoever the ghost is, she is trying to let you in on what happened to Charlotte and her buddies in 1943. I suspect, from your descriptions, that it is Charlotte Wheeler herself. If you think it could help, I would be glad to visit the attic in your great-grandmother's house." Alice frowned. "Would it be possible for me to see the actual letters, and other items you collected from the attic?"

I looked at Ty. "Our schedule is pretty tight now. We have to be in Vermont next week," he said.

"I could meet you at the ferry dock in Bay Shore and pick them up," she offered.

"I think you should meet with my mother first. How about we pick you up at the dock and bring you to Aunt J's, where you can check out all the materials and meet Mom at the same time. I think there is a strong connection between her and the ghost."

"Let's do that. I can't wait to meet your mom, see Jill and meet the ghost. It will be a real tea party!"

"It's settled then," I said. "The only stone left to be turned over is whatever Charlotte's four sister pilots can tell us."

"And maybe those fingerprints can be traced," Doc added. "Which reminds me. Let's talk about what you came here for. He knocked the ash out of his pipe and reached for a large manila folder. "Alice and I have collected a portfolio of material on the topic of espionage and saboteurs as it relates to Long Island, especially during WWII."

Alice was a scholarly researcher. Everything was filed and dated with its source duly noted. She produced a series of news clippings pertaining to U-boat landings at Amagansett, a small town just west of Montauk. Ty and I dove into them immediately.

According to a 1942 article, four men in German uniforms

came ashore from a U-boat. Their purpose was to seek out major manufacturing facilities of war materials and sabotage those plants. They had explosive devices and all the information they needed in order to succeed. But the leader, one George Basch, decided to abandon the plan and turn himself in, providing the FBI with valuable facts about plots the German government had in store for the USA.

Other articles told of frequent sightings of German U-boats. Still, none of the articles claimed that any sabotage plots were successful. *Could our shadowy figure have been a German who made a successful landing and wasn't caught?* I wondered.

"Basch's entire group was caught," Alice said. "But who's to say there weren't other successful landings of spies on our shores? Basch was apprehended because the German sub dropped him off on one of the best patrolled beaches on the east end of Long Island. He was stopped by a Coast Guard patrolman, whom he attempted to bribe. The Coast Guard man, John Cullen, wasted no time reporting the incident. Basch subsequently cooperated with the authorities."

"Then it's possible that a saboteur could have come to Long Island, done some damage, and disappeared? Maybe even rendezvoused with another U-boat?" Ty asked.

"Yes, but we have no proof." Doc sifted through the evidence we had gathered.

"The only piece of hard evidence is the fingerprints

Charlotte picked up, and they most likely won't be on file here in the United States, but in Germany," he concluded.

"Do those records still exist?" Alice asked Doc. "Or were they destroyed in the War? Germany was reduced to rubble by 1945 and the government officials in charge burned a lot of official documents."

Doc's and Alice's research gave us a lot to think about. We grappled with the information, searching for a clue that would help us know for sure what happened in that Grumman plant so long ago.

"Anybody hungry?" Ty asked. "Annie's stomach has been rolling like thunder for an hour now."

"Ty, you are always looking after my best interests," I joked, linking my arm through his.

"I caught a seabass yesterday," Doc said. "Ty, fire up the grill. I'll fry some spuds."

Alice took me by the arm. "C'mon, Annie, let's see if we can muster up enough ingredients for a salad."

"Doc, do you still bake those chocolate chip cookies?" I asked, hoping for the best.

"No cookies, Annie. But, I just baked an apple pie."

"If you weren't so old, Doc, I'd marry you."

"Watch it with the 'old' comments, young lady."

"What about me, Ty, your one and only?" he said, putting his arms around me possessively.

"I don't know, Ty, you'd better take some cooking lessons

from Doc." This teasing felt like the warm fun place I remembered.

We ate in silence, enjoying Doc's fish and chips, and the salad. After dinner we settled into the living room with coffee and pie.

"What's next?" Doc said.

"Wait for Dad to get back with contact information for the Rosies".

"And the prints," Ty added.

"Rosies? Do you mean like *Rosie the Riveter*, the women who built the planes, tanks and other war materiel? You know, Annie, Charlotte and her sister pilots were not the same as *Rosie the Riveter*," Alice said. "The ladies who tested the planes and flew them to air bases were WASPS, the first women in history trained to fly American military aircraft. These were very special ladies. They helped win WWII, and a place for women on the road to equality."

"Yes, Alice. That's right. I guess I take a lot for granted," I said, discovering a lump in my throat. "I'm really proud of Great gramma," was all I could manage.

"Don't forget, young lady, you have those genes," Alice reminded me.

I smiled at Alice, my modern day suffragette.

Alice rose from her chair and, clearing her throat, demanded, "What about this ghost, Annie?"

"I think we'll find her in the attic in New Windsor, Alice. We have to make that happen, and soon."

# CHAPTER 37

## *The Flying Ladies*

"I found your Flying Ladies, Annie." I read Dad's text on the ferry back to Bay Shore, and it was too good to believe.

I called him immediately. "Are they alive, Dad?"

"And kicking. I spoke to each one of them, and they are not only willing to talk to you all, but chomping at the bit to do so."

"Two of them live together in Halesite in a two hundred-year-old house."

"Where is Halesite?"

"It's the northernmost town on Huntington Harbor on Long Island. It goes back to colonial times, and much farther back if you consider the Native Americans on the island. The address is 12 Shore Rd. The phone is 631-242-4243. They're waiting for your call."

"How about the others?"

"Also on Long Island. In assisted living, in Brooklyn,

Bridge Manor, right under the Brooklyn Bridge. Google it. And Annie, take your mother with you. This is really her story as much as it is anyone else's."

"Yeah, Dad. It's the Wheeler women, all of us. I learned a lot about Charlotte's job when we visited Alice and Doc. It really made me proud."

I surprised myself with that annoying lump in my throat. I managed to choke, "Talk to you later, Dad. Bye." The ferry bumped into the slip and we drove home, lost in our thoughts about what the Flying Ladies would tell us.

The next day I called Halesite and Bridge Manor to make appointments for our visits. Then I looked around at the state of my packing for school. I still had a day's worth of work to do. Trouble, the name had stuck, slept on the blue sweater, dreaming about mice or butterflies. Ty had decided the blue sweater was beyond hope and formally gave it to the kitten.

"Christmas is coming, Annie," he had declared.

Ty arrived first, and we had a few moments for a good hug before Mom's tentative knock at the door.

The ride to Halesite in Ty's SUV took over an hour. I took advantage of the time to talk to Mom about "our ghost".

"I think Alice can help us."

"Help how? We don't even know it's a ghost. I do think she is Charlotte though," Mom said.

"I do, too,"

"Me three," Ty added. "Even though I never saw her myself.

Why don't we get Alice to come to New Windsor and introduce her to the lady in the flowered dress?"

"I think that has to happen, Ty. I hope it doesn't make us late getting to school." A silly little lightbulb went off in my head. "I wonder if any of Charlotte's four friends have seen her."

Ty laughed and said, "What are you going to say? By the way, have you seen Charlotte lately, and what do you think of her flowered dress?"

Our laughter died down as we pulled up in front of 12 Shore Rd. There was a note taped to the door.

## DON'T RING BELL
## COME AROUND BACK

We followed a gravel path through dense plantings of hosta and hydrangea mixed with pink roses and black-eyed susans, all showing a last blush of autumn. Bees buzzed and butterflies flitted. A black cat with a white nose darted away and the yapping of a dog acted as a doorbell. We followed the little dog through a French door into a sun room.

"Come in, come in." Two white-haired ladies, one in a wicker chair, the other in a wheelchair, gestured us toward a glass top table with matching ice cream parlor chairs. Two enormous rubber trees towered above us, shading a tinkling waterfall.

"I'm Angie," said the lady in the wheelchair. "And I'm Maxine," said the other lady.

We introduced ourselves and sat down.

"Cassie?" Maxine called into the kitchen. A young girl appeared, a pen stuck behind her ear and a pair of earbuds around her neck.

"Hello. I'm Cassie. I board here. I'm a writer for the local paper and chief cook and bottle washer for the Misses Angie and Maxine." She did a little curtsy in their direction.

We shook hands.

"Will you pour the tea, Cassie, and bring out that cake we made this morning?"

"Sure thing." Cassie slipped through the door to do Maxine's bidding, leaving us to broach the topic at hand.

Mom said, "What a beautiful peaceful place you have here." Maxine and Angie smiled like two Cheshire cats.

"You've come about Charlotte," said Angie.

"And our time working in Bethpage," added Maxine.

"Yes. Did anyone tell you about Brenda McPhee's plane?"

"No one had to, Lovie. We were trying to stop the sabotage, and when Brenda and the plane went missing, we knew it was our saboteur," Angie explained.

"We found out a lot from Charlotte's letters to Frank Bradenton," Mom said. "There was a code at the bottom of each letter. Ty and Annie broke the code. The messages were all about the sabotage."

"We did our best to stop the saboteur. Charlotte risked

her life a few times. Did you know he beat the hell out of her one night?" asked Maxine.

"What was she doing?" Mom demanded.

"Where did he beat her up?" I asked.

"You know, at night the field with the finished planes was blacked out even though the plant went on all night long, twenty-four/seven as they say today. Charlotte discovered the faulty bomb bay door hinge by accident and decided to check the incoming parts." Maxine warmed to her story. Angie shook her head, wringing her hands in her lap.

"That's when she saw him. She had all the women on the assembly line check that hinge part and replace it if it was faulty."

Angie picked up the story. "But then she went a step further and checked the parts carts to see if good parts were being replaced with faulty ones. The carts were kept outside the factory in the darkness of the field."

"That's when he attacked her. If I hadn't played lookout, she'd have been dead." Maxine's voice choked on the last word.

"Why didn't you report what you found to the management of the plant?" Ty asked.

"We didn't know who all was involved!" Angie exclaimed.

"If anyone in management had been involved, we would be toast," Maxine said.

"Look at what happened to Brenda. After she went missing, we decided to keep stopping those faulty parts in their tracks."

"About a week after Brenda's plane went missing and Charlotte was beat up, the saboteur disappeared," Maxine added. "By the way, Charlotte was supposed to be on that plane that went down. Did you know that?"

"Yes, we spoke to Felix Wiedermeier. He worked in the plant and saw what happened when Charlotte missed the plane."

"Why didn't you report the sabotage to the FBI?" Ty asked.

"Same reason, Ty. If the FBI came in, the whistle would be blown on us. Right or wrong, we took matters into our own hands." Angie and Maxine looked from me to Ty to Mom with the most resolute look I'd seen since my fifth grade teacher demanded to know who put the piranha in the goldfish bowl.

"Were you aware of George Basch and the German U-boats that landed off shore at Amagansett?"

"You bet. It was all over the papers. We think that's where our guy came from. He's the one that got away." Angie gave us a knowing look.

"You ladies are quite good detectives," I said. Angie and Maxine exchanged smiles. Maxine nodded and added, "Did you find the fingerprints Charlotte collected?"

You could have knocked me over with a feather. The Flying Ladies knew every part of the story we had been unraveling for days. It was *their* story. We had been right all along. Everything we'd figured out was true!

"Yes, my dad works for the State Department and is trying to track down their owner."

"Will you tell us what you find?

"Absolutely. We think you deserve to know the whole story. You saved a lot of lives," Carol said.

Cassie came out with the cake. There were two numbered birthday candles on top, 96. Mom's jaw dropped open.

"We have a surprise for you," Angie and Maxine said, looking like the piranha that ate the goldfish.

From behind Cassie, two other white haired ladies approached, one with a walker, the other with a cane.

"Connie and Edie?" Mom asked.

"Sure is," said Maxine. "And today is Charlotte's birthday!"

*These were Charlotte's buddies, their bodies now fragile as the bones in a bird's wing, their eyes sharp and bright as a hawk's, their minds treasure troves of memories and wisdom,* I thought. I felt so lucky that we found them.

"We overheard your conversation," said Connie. "There's not much to add. We started working on the production line in the plant. Some of us knew how to fly. When they ran out of men to fly the Avengers to California, we stepped up to the plate. We had to join the WASPS and do some training, and the Army Air Force gave us a good going over for security, but we all passed."

"It was the most exciting time of my life," Edie added. "Just thinking about it makes my heart swell with pride."

"At your age, you'd better be careful," joked Angie.

Cassie was lighting the candles on the cake.

"Shall we blow out the candles for Charlotte?" Maxine gestured for all of us to gather round and we started to sing *Happy Birthday*. Her voice was strong until she got to Charlotte's name. A little quaver spoke volumes about how close these ladies must have been.

We blew out the candles. "Please, cut the cake, Annie. You're the one who must carry on for all of us."

The Flying Ladies looked at each other with some sort of shared knowing. Maxine looked at us and said, "Ty, Annie, Carol. We know this sounds nuts, but have you seen Charlotte in a flowered dress lately?"

# CHAPTER 38

## Alice Meets the Ghost

"Yes," Mom gasped, clutching her throat. "Annie and I have seen what we believe to be the ghost of Charlotte. And yes, in a flowered dress." Mom looked at me, and made a small triumphant thumbs-up.

"We also believe she's led us to two important clues. But we aren't sure what they mean," I said. "Maybe if we compare notes, we can make out what she is trying to tell us."

"This is what I think," Angie said. "Char died in a plane crash well after the war. She never had the satisfaction of finding out exactly who the saboteur was, even though she had strong suspicions. After Frank was killed, if she hadn't had Carla, she would have just drifted away."

At the sound of Carla's name, Maxine clucked and blew through her teeth, looking from Mom to me.

"We know about Charlotte's pregnancy, and how hard it

was when Frank was killed," Mom said. "Carla, my mother, told me a long time ago."

"Charlotte loved Carla. She was all Char had left of Frank, but staying in the present with Carla was a real struggle. Maxine and I visited her as often as possible," Angie added.

"She never got over Brenda's death. She felt guilty," Maxine said.

"She never got over Frank's either," Connie added. "Those first few years, it was painful to be with her. She didn't say much. She just looked like someone had torn her soul out."

*No wonder Charlotte's ghost isn't at peace*, I thought.

"I have an idea. Are you ladies able to travel, like, say, to Maryland?" Mom asked.

"It can be arranged," said Maxine. "We have gone to some ceremonies in Washington, D.C. together, commemorating the WASPS and defense plant workers. We have a gentleman who drives us in a van that takes wheelchairs. What have you got in mind?"

"We know a ghost hunter. She knows about Charlotte and has agreed to come with us to Charlotte's home in New Windsor, Maryland," I explained.

"I want to know why she appeared to us, and to you. What does she want?" What is she trying to tell us?" Mom spoke with conviction. A chill went down my spine. I still find ghosts scary.

"Count us in. Right, girls?" Angie shouted.

The Flying Ladies nodded their assent. A cane banged on the floor.

"Hear! Hear!"

# CHAPTER 39

## *Charlotte and the Flowered Dress*

After a few minutes in the car, Mom broke the silence. "Well, that was interesting. And a bit intimidating. What incredible bravery these women had!"

"Yes. I would like to spend more time with them. I bet they have great stories," I answered.

I felt a little *not of this world*, my head buzzing with all the revelations of the past few days. I kept thinking about my family history. I had known so little about the few relatives I had that this was not only an exciting subject to investigate but an emotional one as well.

As soon as we got home, I called Alice with the news that we had been able to swing a meeting in Maryland with the Flying Ladies and, hopefully, Charlotte.

"Annie, this is a wonderful opportunity to get in touch with your DNA and the story of your female ancestors. I can't wait to meet Charlotte," Alice replied on the other end of the line.

We made a date, confirmed it with Maxine and the others, and agreed to meet in New Windsor the following day. We contacted Tallie, Mom's tenant, and she agreed to be there. After all, she had seen Charlotte, too.

Ty flew me and Mom to the little airport in Carroll County, where the three of us rented a car. We arrived at the Wheeler house in New Windsor at noon, just as the van transporting Charlotte's buddies arrived.

Alice D'Elia had driven with them from New York. She had said, "I'd like to get a feel for them. What was their relationship with Charlotte like? If she's been appearing to them, my guess is she trusts them to do whatever it is she wants."

Tallie led us into the dining room where she'd set the table for a light lunch. Ty went to help Ted, Tallie's husband, set up chairs in the attic.

"Shall we do what we came here for?" Alice looked at us, gesturing toward the stairway. It was a slow process getting the Flying Ladies up the stairs but not one of them complained. Ty and Ted had arranged the chairs in a circle. It was a good thing there was plenty of space.

Thankfully, the weather was cool, because this second floor could get quite hot. It already felt claustrophobic and the air had a funny quality to it, or was it my imagination? Dust motes glittered in the light from the two dormer windows.

The bright bulb hanging from the chain above us cast misshapen shadows all about the room.

Alice, bedecked in spirit crystals, called for quiet and led the group through some calming exercises. She asked that only well-intentioned spirits show themselves to the group.

The air changed again.

Alice began, "I want each of you to tell Charlotte something that you never got the chance to say, or that you would like to tell her again."

After a few minutes, she said, "Maxine, please start, and let's just go to our left."

"I'm sorry I didn't visit you that last Christmas. I wanted to talk to you, but thought I would always have another chance. I should have known better." Maxine looked to her left.

"I'm so sorry you lost Frank," Angie added. On it went down the line.

"Me, too," said Connie.

"You were the best and the bravest," Edie mumbled, stifling a sob.

"What do you want from me?" Mom said.

"I never met you, but this house is full of you." I was surprised to hear this from Tallie who had seen Charlotte as often as I had.

I said, "I wish I had known you. I do have your DNA, and I hope you'll be as proud of me someday as I am of you."

Ty sat silently, holding his tiny camera. A minute went by, then two. We looked at each other. Charlotte, who had made her noisy appearance to us on every visit, seemed to have become shy. Maybe it was because there were so many of us.

Another minute went by. Doubt creased the faces of all the members of the circle. I moved to push my chair back, but Alice put her hand on my forearm. I started to pull away. A door slammed!

Ty, with me hot on his heels, peered around the doorway to the end of the hall, but the door had slammed at the other end. The room was colder all of a sudden. *A sure sign of any self-respecting ghost,* I thought.

We returned to our places in the circle and there she was, transparent as a proper ghost ought to be. I was beginning to realize that this ghost had a little sense of humor.

Her hair formed a blond cloud around her face and the flowered dress swirled around her knees. She wore red platform shoes. She held a photo I had not seen in our search of all that stuff in the attic. It was a picture of her and Frank, in the tropics, maybe Bermuda. Frank had on his Navy dress uniform. She was in the flowered dress.

"What can we do for you, Charlotte?" I miss you so much." Maxine's lips quivered.

"What do you want from me, and from Annie? Do you know Annie?" Mom asked.

Charlotte smiled and a wave of warmth emanated from her apparition.

There was no sound. She kept smiling at us. But I heard her say in my head, "Tell our story. We made a difference. I love you all. I *do* know you, Carol and Annie. Keep the story going."

She started to fade. She blew a kiss. "Happy Landings, Flying Ladies."

"Oh, Charlotte, go in peace," cried Maxine.

"Ite, pacem," Angie repeated.

I smiled at Angie's use of Latin, thinking of the Latin textbook we had used to break the code.

Connie and Edie just cried. "We loved her so. She was so brave and good."

"Did she say anything to any of you?" Ty asked.

"Oh, yes!" we all replied in unison. "Didn't you hear her?"

"Not a word," he replied. Ted shook his head as well.

I held Mom's hand. "Mom, we have to tell her story."

"Yes, and I know just where we can do that."

## CHAPTER 40

### *Writing Another Chapter*

The four WASPS were helped down the stairs to the dining room. The two men put the chairs away and were about to lock the attic door.

"Can I just take one last look?" I begged.

They moved aside and I went in, looking at the trunks and dressers that had occupied me and Mom, as we searched for Charlotte's secrets. "Ted," I called out. "I want to take this dresser. Do you think you and Ty can get it into the van?"

Ted and Ty came up the stairs and looked at the dresser.

"Yeah, this one is small. I brought it up here from the spare room myself. It's pretty light," said Ted.

They wrestled the dresser down the stairs and I stood for a while, just breathing. The air had changed again. No electricity. Just the aura of dust and old wood, and paper. I walked through the door for what would be the last time, locked it, removing the old key. The other times we had visited the attic,

I left feeling shaky and disturbed. Today was different. I felt peaceful. I wiped the remaining tears with my sleeve and went to join the others.

Before the group broke up, Alice and Mom took everyone's information. The plan was to collaborate on a story about Charlotte, Maxine, Angie, Connie and Edie.

"I want to visit with you ladies," I said.

"You had better. We will always want to know what is going on in your life," Angie said.

"And don't leave out how things are going with Ty. He's a keeper," Maxine winked.

"Thanks for giving me Charlotte," I said.

"Thanks for giving *us* Charlotte," Mom added. I put my arm around her.

After much waving and blowing of kisses, even a tear or two, the van rolled away from the curb. We thanked Ted and Tallie, and left for the airport.

The three of us were lost in our own thoughts on the flight home. It isn't every day you see a ghost, much less have one speak directly to you. I checked my texts and there was one from Dad.

"Hey, listen to this," I said. "Dad says Charlotte's prints match a cold case in Suffolk County, New York. A body washed up on a beach in Hampton Bays in 1943. There was no identification on the body and the dental records didn't match anyone in the United States. It was speculated that it was the body of a spy because all the manufacturers' tags were removed from his clothing. He says that when spies couldn't get hold of American clothes they removed the tags from German clothing manufacturers, so as not to blow their cover."

"The last piece falls into place," said Ty. "Doc and Alice had it right. Our shadowy figure *did* come from a German U-boat."

We all fell silent for a few minutes, reviewing the story told by the Flying Ladies and fitting this last piece of information into the mystery.

"Without Charlotte's clues this would still be a cold case. I'm glad we had faith in her."

"What were you and Alice and the four WASPS planning back in New Windsor, Mom?"

"We're going to write Charlotte and her four friends' story. There is a museum in Washington, D.C. that commemorates women in the military. We have enough photos, journals, letters and official documents to warrant a special exhibit about the heroism of this small group of women who foiled a saboteur at one of the most important defense plants in America."

"Sounds like you already have a press release written in your head."

"Actually, it's on paper. I've been busy back here."

"What a great TV special this would make," I said to Ty.

"Or even a movie. What do the ads say? *Coming Soon As a Major Motion Picture!*"

We were approaching Republic Field. The tower cleared

us for landing and we taxied to our spot, a curious Jazz Wiedermeier waiting for us.

"How was your trip?" he asked.

"Have we got a story for your dad," Ty said. "When Annie and I come back to New York for Thanksgiving, we will have to get together."

"Meantime, I will send him the short version," Mom said.

"Thanks for everything, Jazz," Ty said, clapping him on the back.

# CHAPTER 41

## *Goodbyes*

We packed the last of my belongings in the rental truck and went back into the apartment to pick up Trouble. We'd had our farewell dinner the day before. All goodbyes said, Aunt J, Dad and Mom returned to whatever was normal for them. I promised to Skype with Mom.

"You have another guardian angel in Charlotte Wheeler," Ty remarked.

"And we are starting a new adventure, Ty." *What was college going to be like? Was I going to keep Charlotte's story and that of the Flying Ladies going with my chosen field? I guess time will tell,* I thought.

I put Trouble in the carrier. She howled. "Just until we get on our way," I assured her.

Outside, Ty was struggling to close the door of the truck. The dresser from New Windsor seemed to be the problem. Looking at it, I could see the top drawer was slightly open, just an inch, but enough to keep the truck door from closing. I pushed at it to make it close. It wouldn't budge.

"Maybe there's something inside that won't let it close," Ty suggested.

I opened the drawer and a red platform shoe, one of a pair that was resting on a flowered print dress, had wedged itself between the frame of the dresser and the top of the drawer. It took my breath away. I turned to Ty.

"Look, Ty. Another message from Charlotte."

"Not just a message, Annie, a gift."

We climbed into the truck and belted up. I put Trouble on my lap to stop her from howling. Ty started the engine and popped two cans of Coke.

"To Frank and Charlotte," he toasted. Taking my hand and kissing my fingertips, he twisted my ring.

"To Ty and Annie," I replied, twisting my precious ring back.

# AFTERWARD

Annie and Ty go off to college in this Annie Tillery Mystery. Annie starts her college career and Ty continues his graduate studies. Annie becomes a doctor and Ty a research geneticist. Together, in their respective careers, they continue to investigate mysteries both scientific and criminal. Look for Annie and Ty in their future adventures.

Printed in the United States
By Bookmasters